FETISH
- A Novel Written by □
Shameek A. Speight
Copyright © 2012 by Shameek A. Speight
Published by True Glory Publications LLC
ISBN- 13: 978-1480096080
ISBN-10:1480096083
First Edition
Email: shameekspeight199@gmail.com
Follow on Twitter: Bless_45
Facebook: Shameek A. Speight

This novel is a work of fiction. Any resemblances to actual events, real people, living or dead, organization, establishments, locales are products of the author□s imagination. Other names, characters, places, and incidents are used fictitiously.

Cover design/Graphics: www.mariondesigns.com
Editor: Shawnna Robinson

Because of the dynamic nature of the Internet, any Web addresses or links contained in this book may have changed since publication and may no longer be valid. The views expressed in this work are solely those of the author and do not necessarily reflect the views of the publisher and the publisher hereby disclaims any responsibility for them.

<u>DEDICATION</u>

I dedicate this book to a great friend Juicy for believing in me. You always rode for me and I have nothing but love for you.

Acknowledgments:

It has only been the power of God, my lord and savior Jesus Christ that I have been able to persevere through many of the trials I've been dealt in my life. I thank him for giving me the strength to move on.

To my family, my beloved sisters, thank you for believing in me. To my mother, I love you very much. To my aunt, I love you. To my daughter, Niomi, I do all this for you princess. To Shawnna Robinson, you been my right hand pushing me along the way and I love you for it, thank you so much. To all the men and women who are locked up, hold your head up and keep your faith there will be a brighter day. To my niggas in the hood, I told you I could sell books. To Antonio Inch Thomas, thank you for teaching me all about the book game. To all the fans, thank you for all your support. To my Facebook Group, Team True Glory, you're the best, I love every one of you, we're more than a team we're a family.

3

FETISH

Chapter 1

ꞮYes keep doing it like that damn! I love that shit baby!ꞮThe man moaned.

He turned his head around to look at TatianaꞮs beautiful face. There was something about her honey brown skin complexion that turned him on even more.

Tatiana looked at his facial expression twisted up in pleasure and pain, and his dark blue eyes seemed to stare at her with lust mixed with ecstasy. *'Shit I should be used to this, but how in the hell can I? But fuck it if he likes it I love it.'* Tatiana said to herself.

ꞮSwitch, use a different one now, I got used to that one.ꞮThe man moaned.

TatianaꞮs eyes scanned the bed looking at the different sex toys on it next to her. She spotted one she liked and picked up a thick 11 inch funny shaped dildo that had small rubber bumps on it. She then grabs the bottle of K-Y Gel off the bed and squeezes a large amount of it onto the dildo and began to jerk it off once she was completely satisfied it was lubed. She bends over and spreads the man's ass cheeks and slowly forces it into his asshole while trying not to show how disgusted she really was. She smiled and worked it in and out of his rectum while he lays flat on his stomach.

Oh shit! Yes! Work it! Work it! You're the damn best! He screams while arching up his back slightly and jerking off his dick.

You like that huh? Huh? Tatiana screamed while pumping even faster and deeper into him.

Yes baby! Ohhhh! Ugghh! Yes! The man screams as he went into ecstasy and climaxed releasing his load spraying cum all over the sheets and his hand, then collapsed flat onto the bed out of breath.

Tatiana grabs all her sex toys off the bed and stuffs them in her large tan Michael Kors purse. Then wiggles her way back into her Bebe jeans, and puts on her blue matching shirt. She slides into her 4 inch red bottom Louboutin shoes, then walks back over to the bed and kisses him on the forehead.

FETISH

"Okay Paterson I'm out of here." Tatiana said.

"Okay dear, you're the best. The money's in the envelope on the brown dresser." Paterson said and closes his eyes.

Tatiana grabs the envelope and opens it, flipping through the bills making sure all the money was there. She had known Paterson for four years now but business was business and she trusted no one but her younger sister in life.

"Well you have the number, call me when you need me." Tatiana said as her heels clicks while she walks out the room and through the lobby and out the hotel into the parking lot.

She walks to a dark gray s430 Mercedes Benz with her sister Juicy behind the wheel. Tatiana hops in the passenger seat and looks her sister up and down then licks her lips in lust. She pulled Juicy's head close into her and their lips lock as they kiss deeply and passionately. Their tongues danced in each other's mouths. Juicy broke their embrace.

"Shit that didn't take too long. I thought you would be in there for at least two hours or more. You were only in there for 40 minutes.⬜ Juicy stated as she started up the car and pulls off.

⬜Yup forty minutes to make seven hundred dollars plus a tip, and all I had to do is stick things in his ass then go on my way. Then he goⓢ home to his wife and family and they never know how much truly a freak he is. I tell you sister, you need to quit that damn security guard job and do dates with me. I made more than the pay check you get every two weeks and all I had to do is one date and still got four more. Youⓡe a fool for not wanting any of this money and using the power of your pussy.⬜

Juicy shook her head as she continued on driving.

⬜Like I told before Tatiana I fuck men because I want to, not for money.⬜ Juicy replied.

Chapter 2

Sweat covers her body as she tosses and turns.

⬛No! No!⬛She screams then stops.

Joy or better known as Juicy was a nickname that stuck with her that her mother had given her because of her plump cheeks. She was eight years old playing in her room with her new Barbie doll with her sister Tatiana who was ten years old. They giggle and laugh while combing their Barbie dolls hair.

⬛My doll is prettier than yours.⬛ Juicy said in a childlike manner.

Her brown skin complexion seems to glow as an innocent smile spreads across her face.

⬛No mines prettier, you see.⬛ Tatiana said holding her Barbie doll up so Juicy could get a better look.

Their smiles quickly disappears off their faces as their room door opens and Dustin their mother's boyfriend stood in the doorway wearing a white tank top and grey sweatpants with a twisted smile, showing his stained yellow teeth from smoking to many cigarettes and drinking straight black coffee. His skinny frame of a body seemed to barely hold his clothes on. His nappy hair on his head and face looked as if he hadn't seen a barbershop or comb and brush in years. Both Juicy and Tatiana drop their Barbie dolls and wrap their arms around each other as tears stream down their cheeks.

"Your mother went to work. You know what that means. When the cats away the mouse will come out to play." Dustin said as he grins with a twisted smile.

"No! We don't want to play that game anymore!" Tatiana said while crying.

"Shut up! You will play my game and like it! Do you understand me?" Dustin yelled as he walks deeper into the room slamming the door shut behind him causing Juicy and Tatiana to jump out of fear.

"Now kiss each other like the way I showed you!" Dustin ordered.

"No! We don't want to play your game anymore, it hurts us and it's wrong. I'll tell my mommy on you!☐ Juicy shouted in a childlike manner.

Dustin walks straight up to her and slaps her and then Tatiana, so hard their necks twisted and little bodies fall off the bed.

☐Ahhhh! Ahhhh!☐ They both scream in pain and began to cry hysterically.

☐Both of you, shut up and sit back on the bed, or I☐l really do something that will really make you cry!☐Dustin shouted as he raises his hand high ready to hit them once more.

Tatiana lifts herself up off the floor and wipes her tears away with her small hands and did the same to Juicy☐s face and helps her up. They both ease back onto the bed.

☐Now kiss and rub each other☐s bodies like I taught you!☐He shouted.

As Tatiana and Juicy slowly start to kiss each other he grins as he pulls down his sweatpants and steps out of them, leaving him standing there in his blue boxer briefs with his right hands in his underwear jerking off his dick back and forth.

☐Yes like that. Now kiss her on the neck. Yeah like that.☐ Dustin said as he became more aroused at watching them kissing and fondling each other's bodies.

He walks over to the bed and pushes Tatiana down and starts removing her clothes, tossing them on the floor. Tatiana knew what was going to happen next as she fought back her tears and wanted to scream. Juicy lay next to her and close her eyes while crying then held Tatiana's hand as Dustin made his way into her, ripping open her tiny vagina. Tatiana cried and screamed in agony and pain as he thrusts in and out of her. She turns her head to look at Juicy who was feeling her pain and crying as well. Dustin pulls out of Tatiana then rips Juicy's clothes off. Then force his way inside her. She screamed and hollered.

Mommy, make him stop, he's hurting me. She screamed repeatedly while holding her sister's hand. Dustin had his way with both little girls for an hour and a half straight before he releases his load and forces them to sit in the bathtub in hot water together. Washing off evidence and any traces of what he had done off of them. Then he left them in their room on the bed. Tatiana held Juicy as she cried the loudest and the longest.

Heather felt the strain on her body after a long day as she walks into her apartment. She was a heavy set woman with a light brown skin complexion.

Lord it feels so good to be home. She said out loud as the smell of food hit her nostrils.

She made her way into the kitchen to see Dustin cooking.

Awwww, baby youre the best. she said as she wraps her arms around him from the back and looks at the pots on the stoves.

How were the girls today? I know you cant wait until the summer is over so they can start school again. I appreciate you watching them all the time until then. Did they behave themselves baby? Heather asks while kissing on his neck and then nibbles on his left ear.

Yeah they were good girls all day. I never have a problem watching your daughters. You know I look at them as if they were my own flesh and blood. Dustin said as he turns around and took her into his skinny arms and kisses her deeply and passionately.

FETISH

"Mmmm!"Heather moans as she felt her clit throbbing.

"Baby stop, your making me wet and I'm horny as hell and the girls are still up." She mumbled in between breathing hard in lust as Dustin eases her on top of the kitchen table slowly kissing down her neck.

"Don't worry they're asleep and won't get up until we call them for dinner." Dustin replied.

"Mmmm, damn baby you know my neck is my spot." She moaned as he continues to kiss and suck on her neck at the same time.

"Shit this is just so fucking sexy." Heather moaned as he unbuttons her blouse and removes her size "DD"breast from her bra, taking her left nipple into his mouth.

"Mmmm tastes sweeter then honey baby." He moaned as his tongue travels all around her body, teasing her and sending chills through her body, making her pussy even wetter.

She braces herself with the palms of her hands on the table while leaning her head back in ecstasy. Dustin gently rubs her throbbing pussy in a circle motion as he raises her skirt up high to her waist he pulled her panties to the side and pulls down his grey sweatpants, letting them drop to his ankles, along with his boxer briefs. He took out his long skinny dick and slowly inserts the tip of it inside her wet box while kissing her lips, working his way deeper inside her with each stroke.

Mmmm, yeah baby, work that dick inside me, this is your pussy. Heather moaned.

'Shit her pussy and daughters pussy feel so damn sweet.' Dustin thought to himself as he picks up his pace.

Ohhh! Ayyye! Ooowee yes! Yes, just like that! She screams as he grinds inside her hitting her G-spot.

Her palms became sweaty and cause her to lose her grip, and now she was lying flat on the table with her legs spread wide open up in the air.

Juicy and Tatiana heard their mothers screams. They wipe their tears away and got off the bed. Their bedroom door was right next to the kitchen. Tatiana opened the door with Juicy by her side to see Dustin pumping in and out of their mother like a mad man. He looks up between Heather's legs to see Juicy and Tatiana standing in their room doorway. He smiles showing his stained teeth and licks his lips.

Ummm. He groans as he thrusts faster and harder while staring at them.

Ugghh! Ohhh! He groans as he releases his load inside of Heather, then mumbles you're next to Juicy and Tatiana who bodies tremble out of fear and ran back into their room.

Damn baby, that was good. Heather moaned. Okay, let me go take a shower and clean myself up while you finish up dinner. You're such a great man baby I'm so happy to have you in my life. She said and then walks off.

A half hour later, Heather walks into the kitchen to see Dustin setting the table. She kisses him on the cheek and smiles with joy, and then made her way to Juicy and Tatiana's room. She opens the door and walks in, shutting it behind her to see Tatiana and Juicy holding each other crying on the bed.

FETISH

"Girls, what's wrong?" Heather asked in a concern worried tone and sat on the edge of their bed looking at her children with a worried heart and a confused look on her face.

She moved closer to them and gently touches both of their heads, playing in their hair.

"Please my babies, tell me what's wrong?" Heather said while crying.

"Mommy I have to tell you something." Juicy said with tears streaming down her cheeks.

"No Juicy don't! Damn, you're only going to make it worst!" Tatiana shouted while wiping her own tears away.

"Tatiana you be quite child and shut your mouth. Juicy tell me what's going on." Heather replied.

Juicy sniffs the running snot that was dripping down her nose onto her top lip.

Mommy Dustin hurts us every time you go to work. He makes us play nasty games we don't like." Juicy said while looking her mother in the eyes.

FETISH

⬛What do you mean baby he hurt you and your sister? And what games he makes you play that you don⬛t like dear?⬛ Heather asks.

Juicy⬛s lips trembles before she spoke.

He touches us down there mommy.⬛ Juicy said pointing to her private area. He put his thing inside us mommy and it hurts real bad, it makes me bleed down there. I scream and cry and tell him to stop but he hit me and Tatiana mommy, and then makes us take a bath before you come home. He does it every day when you leave. He hurts us mommy. Don⬛t leave us with him no more. Please mommy.⬛Juicy said while crying hysterically.

Heather looks at both her daughters with a stunned look on her face. Then her facial expression changes and balls up into anger and rage.

⬛This can⬛t be true! You⬛re lying!⬛ She shouted.

⬛No mommy I⬛m not lying, it⬛s true. Look, see.⬛ Juicy said while pulling down her jean shorts and showing her mother the inside of her hello kitty panties where blood stains were from her spotting because Dustin had torn and ripped her womb.

Heather's body shook and she shakes her head from side to side as tears watered up in her eyes.

"Whack!" "Whack!" Out of nowhere Heather slaps Juicy and Tatiana so hard their brown skin bruised up and turns dark blue, leaving her hand print.

"Mommy, what did we do?" Juicy cried out.

"Listen here you little bitches. You're lying, my man didn't touch y'all. What would he want with little girls when he got me? I never want to hear you say he touched you again or tell no one outside this apartment your lies. Are we clear?" Heather shouted.

Tatiana just stared at her mother with hate in her eyes as she rubs her face with her little hand.

"But mommy we're not lying, he touches us and hurts us really bad, all the time, I swear." Juicy replied while crying and not understanding why her mother wouldn't believe her.

FETISH

"Whack!" Her words cause her to get slapped two more time.

Heather was about to hit her once more as she crawled up into a tight tiny ball and Tatiana jumps on top of her, covering her body, using her own body as a shield as her mother's hand came crashing down on the center of her back, slapping it hard.

"Ahhhh! Ahhhh!" Tatiana hollered in excruciating pain from the sting of the blow that traveled through her little body.

"Listen up you little heifers; both of your fathers were no good bum ass niggas that left. Now I'm stuck raising two children by my goddamn self with no help and no fucking child support. No good man wants a woman with two children that have two different fathers at that. Your own damn fathers don't want your asses, I take care of you. Now that I finally got a man that makes me happy and wants me, even with you two heifers and y'all want to ruin it. Hell fucking no! You won't mess this up for me. I'm in love, Dustin is a great man, and he puts food in this house, helps out with the bills with his Social Security checks and loves me only. You will never bring up this shit you told me again. Do you hear me young ladies!"

Heather said while crying and hitting her daughters with an open palm on their backs and legs.

Tatiana took most of the blows for Juicy as they cried together. Twenty minutes later, Heather exits their room, leaving them on their beds crying.

What was all that about? Dustin asked as she walks into the kitchen.

Nothing baby, don't concern yourself about it. She replied while kissing him.

I love you Dustin.

I love you too girl. He replied.

So you're not going call the girls out to eat, the food is ready and the table is set. Dustin said.

No they're not going to eat tonight. They will stay in their room for acting up and telling lies, but you and I are going in our room and finish what we started earlier. I'm going to get your dick up and put it down over and over until you can't get it up any more. Heather said while holding him by the hand and leading him into the bedroom.

I like the sound of that. He said while smiling as his dick grows inch by inch in his sweatpants.

Tatiana had stopped crying and knew she had to be the strong one and held Juicy who had tears streaming down her face.

I told you Juicy not to tell her, she don't care what happens to us and don't want us to mess up what she has with that mean man. Tatiana said.

But does that mean she loves him more than us? Juicy said in a childlike manner.

Yes it does little sister. Tatiana replied.

Juicy and Tatiana cried themselves into a deep sleep. In the middle of the night the sound of the door creeping open made Tatiana pop up out her sleep in fear as her heart race, to see the door shut and Dustin walking into the dark room.

I told you two not to talk about our games, now it will be even worse. He said in a whisper as he walks closer.

No, please, no mommy! Tatiana cried and her little body trembles.

"Don't worry you're last." He said as he climbs on top of Juicy who was sound asleep.

The feeling of her pink hello kitty nightgown being lifted up and panties being ripped off woke her up along with the pain of something being forced inside her womb, made her eyes open wide and start screaming but to only have a large hand cover her mouth and half her face as Dustin pumps in and out of her.

"No! No! Nooo!" Juicy screams over and over. "Nooo!" As tears run down the side of her face onto the bed.

"Shhh!" Juicy get up! Get up please!" Tatiana said softly and shook her sister.

"No God please no!" Juicy screams and cried in her sleep then opens her eyes and looks around scanning her environment.

Juicy calm down it was just a dream your safe now, I got you." Tatiana said as she wraps her arms around her.

"No you're wrong Tatiana. It wasn't just a dream or a nightmare. I felt him inside me all over again. I felt his hand covering my mouth and mommy beating us, telling us not to tell and that we're lying." Juicy said while crying.

"No little sister we're no longer children anymore and we're much stronger, it's us against the world okay." Tatiana said as she wipes Juicy's tears away and lifts up her chin then stares into her eyes.

"We're safe now, I made sure of that." She said as she presses her lips against Juicy's and slowly opens her mouth, kissing her deeply and passionately.

They moan with each kiss as their hands slowly roam each other's bodies just as they use to do as children.

"Damn Juicy, I love the fact you sleep naked. It gives me easy access." Tatiana said while giggling then slowly places wet intense kisses on her neck.

"Mmmm!" Juicy moans as each kiss sends a sweet sensation through her body, making her clit throb.

Tatiana's lips travel down to her collar bone of her neck then her tongue slowly travels to her left breast and gently and seductively took her nipple into her mouth while moaning

Mmmm! She moans with each suck she took then let the tip of her tongue travel around her nipple in a circular motion.

Then she grabs Juicy's right breast and does the same thing, taking turns sucking both of her nipples. The sensation drives Juicy into ecstasy as it teases and pleases her at the same time. She looks down at Tatiana's head moving from side to side and twisting. The sexy sight only turns her on even more.

Ohhh! Damn Tatiana you're making me wet as hell. Juicy moaned as her body quivers with the thought of Tatiana's tongue on her clit.

Damn Tatiana, stop fucking teasing me. Juicy moaned as Tatiana places slow kisses down her stomach then onto her thick brown thighs.

She spreads Juicy's legs while looking up at her. Their eyes connected and never left each other, making them both moist between their legs.

Mmmm, shit! Juicy moans as Tatiana's tongue lightly touches her clit.

Damn lick it just like that. Juicy moaned as she winds her hips while holding

24

the back of Tatiana's head, as her head twists from side to side. She lets the tip of her tongue flick up and down on Juicy's pussy then took her pussy lips into her mouth gently sucking on them

"Ohhh! Ayeee! Ahhh! Ohhh yesssss!" Juicy moans while making a hissing sound with her mouth wide open.

"It's us against the world Juicy, all we need is each other." Tatiana said in between sucking and licking.

She looks up at Juicy with a long string of spit mix with cum hanging from her bottom lip, as she crawls toward Juicy's face and they kiss seductively.

"Mmmm." They both moan.

Juicy broke their embrace and pushes Tatiana's head back down in between her legs. I want to cum, Tatiana make me cum." Juicy said in a horny tone.

Tatiana smiles as she works her magic taking Juicy's clit into her mouth sucking it like it tastes sweeter than honey.

"Mmmm you taste so fucking sweet." She moaned while sucking and licking her clit then pushes Juicy legs up into the air and works her tongue inside her wet-box.

Ohhaaa! Ayeee! Yesss! Damn yes! Juicy screams as her hands roam her breast squeezing them firmly and pinching her nipples as sweet juices flow out of her.

Tatiana swallows all her sweet juices and continues to stick her tongue in and out of her wet-box.

Mmmm! God! Ohhh I'm fucking cumin! Ughhh! Juicy screams as load as she could and grips the sheets with her fingers as she climax, sending a rush of cum into Tatiana's mouth.

She swallows it all and continues to lick her clit. Juicy's body quivers in ecstasy. Tatiana lifts her head up and smiles between Juicy's legs while licking her lips. She inches her way up and stood on the sole of her feet on the bed while squatting lowering herself on top of Juicy's face. Juicy wasted no time to go to work. She grabs Tatiana's ass cheeks palming them while squeezing them and working her tongue back and forth on her clit and pussy hole, then taking her pussy lips all the way into her mouth.

Oh Lord! Fuck! Just like that suck it. Tatiana moaned while breathing hard as she used the palms of her hands to brace onto the wall as she rocks her hips.

Oh God! Tatiana screams as tears of pleasure run down her face.

Oooweee! Ohhh God! She screams as her body shook and her fluids stream out of her into Juicy's mouth.

Juicy licks it up while switching up from sucking her clit. Juicy tries to gasp for air as cum flows down her throat and the side of her face. Tatiana was lost in ecstasy, she starts to rub her pussy all over Juicy's lips and chin and nose.

Damn! She screams as she collapsed on the side of the bed next to Juicy breathing hard.

Juicy wipes Tatiana's cum from her face with her sheet and then sticks her fingers into her mouth sucking them.

Mmmm! Damn, I love the way you taste sis. She said.

FETISH

⌐Good because I want more.☐ Tatiana said while rubbing her clit and inserting two fingers into her wet-box.

Juicy grins and they went back at it for the rest of the night.

Chapter 3

Juicy sniffs the air. ⬜Mmmm⬜ and moans in her sleep. Her stomach growls from hungry. The smell of grits, eggs and bacon linger in the air. She yarns and stretches out her arms. She then reaches over to the next side of her bed to see that Tatiana wasn⬜t there. Just a large wet spot of dried up cum on the sheet from the loving they had made. The sun shined in her room, brightening it up. ⬜Grrrr⬜ her stomach made a funny sound.

⬜Okay! Okay! I hear you. I⬜m getting up now. Like how in the hell is my own stomach going to control me.⬜ Juicy said out loud to herself as she eases out of her bed and walks to her closet and pulls out a pink silk bathrobe and puts it on. Then she slides on her pink fury slippers. She walks out her bedroom and down the stairs to the first floor. Voices could be heard coming from the dining room. Juicy enters the dining room with an innocent smile on her face as she sees Shanelle and Kandy at the marble table eating.

Shanelle was Trinidadian with a dark sexy chocolate skin complexion; her long weave was 20 inches long that came down to her ass. Everything about her screams sex, she was a slim built with a plump ass.

Kandy or Kandy Cola as she likes to be called, because of her Coca Cola bottle shaped body, was a light brown skin complexion. Her appearance was perfect she had the face of an angel but the mind of a true gold digger. DD size breast and the perfect waist line. Her stomach was flat with a four pack abs. Her thighs were thicker than any woman Juicy had seen. Then there was her ass that Juicy swore up and down was fake, because there was no human way possible for a woman s ass to be so voluptuous, so thick and perfect and sits up right without her having an ounce of body fat on her besides her thighs and butt cheeks. One look at Kandy-Cola men went crazy with lust, she was the type of woman you would never see in person only in your dreams or on T.V or in magazines. Men threw themselves at her feet and did whatever she desired.

 Good morning Juicy booty. Shanelle said in a joking manner.

 Good morning skinny fatty heifer. Juicy replied while laughing.

FETISH

"Hey miss perfect body." Juicy said to Kandy-Cola.

"Hey girl," Kandy-Cola said while never looking up from her plate of food. "You're just mad my butts bigger than yours and I can make it clap." Kandy-Cola said with a smile on her face as she stood up and turns around making her fat ass cheeks clap in Juicy's face, only wearing white booty shorts.

"I like looking at your ass more than mines." Juicy said as she grabs Kandy-Cola's ass then slaps it. "That shit fake anyway, it's too perfect." Juicy said.

"My ass isn't fake it sure the hell doesn't feel like it and if it was, shit, the niggas don't know or care, because they don't stop blowing up a bitch phone, fiending for some Kandy-Cola." Kandy-Cola said causing all the women to laugh.

"Enough playing around, it's time to pay up, bills and vacation money." Tatiana said as she walks out the kitchen with two plates in her hands. One for Juicy and the next for herself, she was only wearing a blue thong with the matching lace bra.

FETISH

She sat Juicy's plate in front of her and took a seat at the head of the table.

"As you all know the Bike Fest is coming up and so is Labor Day, so those are more days to earn extra money for our cruise trip to the Bahamas and then our trip to Las Vegas. So we all get to put into the pot, so give it up with your share of mortgage money bitches. It's the first of the month."

Kandy-Cola digs into her Michael Kors purse that was on the marble kitchen table and began counting a stack of hundred dollar bills. "Here's $1,500." She said passing it to Tatiana. "I forgot to tell y'all I was messing with a sexy ass new rapper Lucci and girl that nigga love eating some coochie and spending every dime he has to get a taste of my shit." Kandy-Cola said as she rolls her neck and licks her lips as she counted more stacks of money.

"Bitch you're too much, you're always fucking a rapper or someone in the entertainment industry." Tatiana said as she counts the money Kandy-Cola passed to her.

"They should've listened to their mothers, it's so true, never trust a woman with a big ole ass and a pretty smile." Kandy-Cola said causing the other three women to bust out laughing.

"Girl I don't know why you just don't stick with Roger's corny ass. He makes decent money working for M.T.A. and loves you and knows everything about your ass. The good, the bad and tricks you do."Juicy stated.

"Schmmp!"Kandy-Cola sucks her teeth. "Heifer please, Roger is too much of a bug-a-boo and too goodie good. I like and need a thug, a tough rough nigga that will put me in my place, smack my ass and pull my weave, that covers my tattoos. Hmmm, and most of all a bank account filled with money. There isn't anything sexier than that. Just thinking about it got my pussy wet and throbbing."Kandy-Cola replied.

"Amen to that." Shanelle and Tatiana said agreeing with her and getting turned on with the thought of a thug life businessman deep inside them.

"Besides Roger is so pussy whipped he's not going anywhere, it's been six years and his butt is still around knowing I be getting dick down by other men, but all those fools have to pay to have a bad bitch like me in their world. I treat them like accessories and change them when they don't match my outfit." Kandy-Cola said causing them all to bust out laughing once more.

"Bitch you're too much for your own good." Shanelle said as she digs in her purse and passes Tatiana a stack of money. There's $1,200 there. I'll have more to add to the pot at the end of the week when I hit up this next nigga for abortion money. Shanelle stated.

"Shanelle you are the only one I know who still pulls that abortion scam on men and I'm shocked it works, but your ass really does get pregnant, and more than a damn cat in heat. I thought the scam was to lie and say you're pregnant and collect the money, but you get pregnant every two months for real. I lost count on how many abortions you had girl after number seven." Juicy said and Kandy-Cola and Tatiana bust out laughing.

"Schmmp!" Shanelle sucks her teeth. "Please! At least I make money and can bring something to the table. You need to stop acting all high and mighty. You're a nymph just like the rest of us, and love's some dick all the time and your pussy licked. The only difference between us is that we get money from any nigga touching our goodies while you fucking

men for free and don't have shit to show for it.
Shanelle spitted out then rolls her eyes, and
then her eyes met Tatiana's, who gave her an
angry stare and facial expression read bitch I'll
beat your ass if you make my sister cry.

Shanelle stares back at Tatiana. Don't
look at me that way. Shanelle said while trying
to match her look.

It's okay Tatiana. Shanelle was just
speaking her mind. You know she can never
control her mouth it's always been like that, but
like I said many times over to every one of you
in this house. I love y'all and don't knock what
you do for a living and getting money, but that
scamming shit isn't for me and I want to be a
writer, a novelist one day. There's no price on
my pussy. It's too good to set a price on, this
pussy is priceless, so if I fuck a man it's
because I want to. Juicy said then continues
eating her girts and eggs with cheese.

Okay, enough money talk, we have a
full day ahead of us. Juicy I need you to pick
me up around 5pm when I get out of school I
have five dates set up. Tatiana said.

But sis, I might get out of work late
around four, so coming from the city to

Brooklyn at rush hour I won't make it to you in an hour. Juicy replied.

Juicy you know I hate to be late to making money and that's the only rule I have about you taking my car baby girl.

Ugghhh! Juicy sighs and holds her head in stress.

Tatiana gets up out her chair and walks over to Juicy and lifts up her chin, then lightly kiss her lips. From the corner of her eyes she looks at Shanelle and Kandy-Cola and grins. A big Kool-Aid smile spreads across Kandy-Cola's face as she stood up and lust went through all four of the woman's bodies, as they watch Kandy-Cola take off her bra showing off her perfect sized double CC breast, and her four pack abs on her stomach and voluptuous thick thighs that had tattoos running all down them. She walks over to Juicy and bends over and starts sucking on her while gently rubbing her breast.

Tatiana slides Juicy's robe open.

Shhh mmmm shit! Juicy moans as Kandy-Cola takes her left nipple into her mouth, then Tatiana took her right nipple into her mouth gently nibbles on it.

FETISH

⟦Damn!⟧Juicy said as she held onto the back of both their heads as it twisted from side to side and they seductively licks and sucks her nipples.

Shanelle stood up and removes the shirt she had on and slides off her short jean skirt. She never wears panties or bras, so she was butt naked in a matter of seconds. Then seductively walks over to them. She drops to her knees in front of Juicy and spread her legs and slowly and intensely kisses her inner thighs, inching her lips closer to Juicy⟧s clit.

The sensation of all three of their lips on her body made it quiver as she sticks her own fingers in to her mouth and begins sucking on them.

⟦Mmmm⟧ Lord!⟧ Juicy said as Shanelle⟧s lips finally met her clit.

Juicy knew Shanelle had a mouth on her and was known for talking shit to everyone, but knew how to work her thick full lips.

⟦Mmmm! Yeaaa! Mmmm!⟧ Shanelle moaned as she kisses Juicy⟧s clit over and over, then let⟧s her tongue travel around it, tongue kissing her clit deeply and passionately.

Oh shit! Oooweee! Yesss! Yesss!
Juicy screamed.

Tatiana lifts her head up and Kandy-Cola did the same, their lips met. Tatiana broke their embrace.

Bend that ass over. Tatiana ordered.

Kandy-Cola smiles with lust in her eyes as she bends over onto the table. Tatiana eases over to her leaving Juicy stuck in ecstasy with Shanelle between her legs. Tatiana pulls down Kandy-Cola's white lace boy short panties and stood there stuck, looking at her amazing voluptuous ass that had a dragon tattoo on one butt cheek and a tiger on her right butt cheek. Kandy-Cola looked back at Tatiana.

So are you just going stare at it as if you don't know what to do with it. She said while letting her tongue travel across her lips.

No, I know what to do with that ass it's just so damn perfect. Tatiana said then slaps it and watches it shake.

Then Kandy-Cola bounces it up and down like a stripper making her ass cheeks claps. Tatiana got on her knees and spreads

Kandy-Cola's voluptuous perfect ass cheeks apart and uses her index finger to play with her clit. The teasing sensation made Kandy-Cola's pussy wet, soaking her fat thick pussy lips. Tatiana inserts two fingers inside Kandy-Cola's wet-box.

"Ummm! Mmmm!" Kandy-Cola moans as Tatiana works her fingers back and forth and tapping the top walls of her vagina.

"Mmmm! Shhhh" Shittt! You always know how to work my G-spot." Kandy-Cola moaned while making a hissing sound as her juices drip from her wet-box.

"Mmmm, is that so?" Tatiana replied as she slowly sticks out her tongue and lets it travel from Kandy-Cola's clit to her pussy hole, giving her nice long licks repeatedly. Then flicks her tongue up and down on her clit and then sucks it.

"Damn!" Kandy-Cola moans as her facial expression twists up into pleasure as she bangs her fist on the table as Tatiana's tongue slips inside her and she began to lick the sensitive walls of her vagina.

"Fuck me!" Kandy-Cola screamed while biting her bottom lip.

FETISH

She arches her back and sticks her butt out even more as Tatiana devours her slowly from her pussy hole to her clit. She tongue kisses Kandy-Cola's asshole then stuck her tongue inside it, fucking her with it as her fingers work faster and harder inside her, hitting her spot.

"Ahhhh! Mmmm!" Kandy-Cola screams in ecstasy as cum rushes out of her and her body quivers and jerks.

"Damn Tatiana." She moans, out of breath and could hear slurping sounds echo through the room as Juicy switch places with Shanelle and had her sitting on the chair with her legs spread wide open and lift up pushed to her breast as Juicy tongue kisses her love box.

She moans in joy with her facial expression balled up as she watches a long string of saliva mixed with cum hang from Juicy's bottom lip as she pulls away. The sight of it only made Shanelle wetter making her pussy leak juices, soaking the chair then dripping into Juicy's mouth and down her breast as she took her clit into her mouth once more.

FETISH

"Ayyye! Ayyye! Ohhhh! Yesss! Fuck yesss!" Shanelle screams as she had an orgasm and climaxed for the third time.

Two hours later all four women laid on the dining room floor out of breath with their pussy's soaking wet from cumin more times than they could count.

"Oh shit I'm late for work!" Juicy said while easing off the floor. Tatiana bust out laughing along with Kandy-Cola and Shanelle.

"If you quit your 9 to 5 damn job and get money like the rest of us you wouldn't worry about being late or not, because a nigga going to pay for your time, but you can't front this was worth your ass being late wasn't it?" Tatiana said.

"Whatever!" Juicy replied with a smile on her face as she ran naked up the stairs to the shower.

"That woman will never open her eyes and see the power she has between her legs." Kandy-Cola said.

"Oh she will, I'll make sure of it. Just give it sometime." Tatiana replied as Shanelle

and Kandy-Cola lay on top of her and she
played in their hair.

Chapter 4

Kandy-Cola steps out of the Far Rockaway Houses dressed in an all-white tight fitted Chanel shirt that did little to hide her perky double ⌐CC⌐breast and a pair of all white Givenchy jeans that hugged her hips and ass and black Jimmy Choo high heels that had white stubs on the sides of them. She walks to her white 2009 Range Rover truck that was parked on the street.

⌐Cola!⌐

Kandy-Cola stopped dead in her tracks as she heard someone call out her name.

⌐Schmmp!⌐Kandy-Cola sucks her teeth, because she had recognized the voice right away. She stomps her foot and turns around to face a jade green color Hummer truck with the passenger window rolled down.

⌐What do you want Roger?⌐ She shouted while snapping her finger.

Roger adjusts his seeing glasses on his face.

FETISH

"Why haven't you answered any of my calls? Cola you already know what I want. It's you baby." Roger replied.

"Listen Roger, I don't have time for this, I have moves to make and things to do." Kandy-Cola shouted with her hands on her hips.

"That's how you're going to treat me after all I did for you?" Roger shouted back.

Kandy-Cola knew where the conversation was heading and didn't want everybody in the street in her business. She opens the Hummer's passenger side door and steps inside and sat down, then rolls up the window.

"What the fuck is your problem? You're not my man, for me to be reporting too. I don't need you popping up in front of my house with your loud ass mouth spreading my business." Kandy-Cola said while looking him in the eyes.

She had to admit to herself that he was a sexy and handsome man in his three piece suit. He had a dark gray, brown skinned complexion that seemed to glow, and had shiny wavy hair and a well-trimmed beard and goat-t.

FETISH

"Cola stop treating me like one of your damn groupies or a fan from Facebook or Twitter, it's me. We been dealing with each other for six years before you got all conceited and thinking you're too good for me or feel like rappers, singers and entertainers are worth your time. They're only using you for your body, that's it! But I love you no matter what." Roger said sincerely.

"Roger, I told your ass I'll make time for you when I can and don't be showing up to my house uninvited or you might see something that will break that little heart of yours." Kandy-Cola said as she prepares to get out the truck.

Roger grabs her by the arm stopping her.

"I can't believe you're doing this to us. I've been here for you from day one. I got you that damn Ranger Rover you're driving. I pay for the car notes and invested over $60,000 into you alone and you're trying to play me. I fucking made you!" Roger shouted with spit flying out of his mouth onto his suit.

Kandy-Cola yanked away, freeing herself from his grip on her arm.

FETISH

Let's get a few things straight. Last I checked, God and my mother made me and gave me life, yes you may have gotten the truck for me and the loan in your name but the tittle and paper work to the truck is in my name and I don't need you to pay the note you choose too, I got this. Kandy-Cola said sarcastically.

Cola I didn't mean it like that or to upset you. Roger pleaded.

Hold up I'm not done speaking, you spend on me is nothing compared to what all the ballers in the entertainment industry throw my way and if you was a real man you wouldn't have a loan out for my truck you would've paid for it straight up! Kandy-Cola shouted and steps out the Hummer and slams the door, then unlocks her Ranger Rover and hops in.

Cola I didn't mean it like that. I just need to spend time with you. I love and miss you. Roger stated.

Kandy-Cola rolls down her driver's side window as she starts her truck to pull off. She grabs her Channel sunglasses off the passenger's seat and puts them on and stares at him with a disgusting look on her face.

FETISH

"When you're done acting the fuck up and ready to listen and only come when I call you and you're ready to spend some real money on me, then we can spend time together." Kandy-Cola said.

"Wait Cola, let me take you shopping!" Roger shouted.

Kandy-Cola steps on her breaks, looks at Roger, and a smile spreads across her face.

"So how much you're trying to spend on me?" She replied.

"I'll say $6,000, a little more. Or until my Chase Credit Card is maxed out." Roger replied.

Kandy-Cola checks the diamond studded watch on her wrist that read 10:00 a.m.

'Damn I have to meet Casino-Rich, but he's not even up yet. I was just going to surprise him and work him over and get what I want, but six thousand is chump change, but what bitch will be foolish enough to turn down a free shopping spree.' Kandy-Cola thought to herself.

FETISH

"Okay I'm down, but don't think you're going to get any pussy just because you're blowing a little bit of money on me and you have to drop me back off at my house as soon as we're done. Is that clear?" Kandy-Cola said as she rolled up her window and steps out her truck, hitting the alarm behind herself and hops in the passenger seat of the jade green Hummer.

"You have my word Cola. I'll follow your rules baby." Roger replied while smiling like the cat that swallowed the canary as he pulls off heading out of Queens to Fifth Avenue in Manhattan.

After spending four thousand dollars in the Gucci store and another five thousand in the Louis Vuitton store. Kandy-Cola then maxes out the last two thousand on Roger's credit card in H&M on shirts and blouses and some jeans. She figures she would mix some of the designer labels with the others to give it her own twist.

Kandy-Cola's teeth were sunk deep into the pillow with her face down and her ass up in the air.

'Damn how the hell did I let myself end back up at his place, and in the Bronx at that.

FETISH

Damn, I might as well get my nut and let him get his shit off it's the least I can do for him taking me shopping and me maxing out his credit card.' She thought to herself.

Mmmm yes. She moaned into the pillow with each stroke he gave her.

He caresses her back with his hands, then makes his way to her voluptuous ass and slaps it repeatedly, watching the tattoo of the red and purple dragon shake.

Shhh Yes shit! Mmmm! Ohhh fuck! Stick it in my ass! Fuck me in my ass! She shouted while lifting her head up from the pillow and looks back at him.

'Damn even though he don't have no real money, I can't even front he's sexy as hell.' Kandy-Cola thought to herself as she stares at Roger's brown skin complexion and slim muscled up body.

Sweat drips down from his forehead and splashes onto her ass cheeks. Roger pulls out his seven inch soaking dick from her sweet juices and jerks it back and forth. He then taps the head of it onto each ass cheeks.

"How bad do you want it? Beg for it."
He said through clenched teeth.

"Damn baby stop! Don't play with me!
Fuck this tight asshole." Kandy-Cola moans in
lust while winding her hips and pressing her
ass against his pelvis area.

"You want this dick don't you?" Roger
teases as he puts the tip of his dick in her
vagina and pulls it out repeatedly, sending a
sweet chill through her body, making her pussy
throb and jump.

"Roger, stop fucking playing with me,
alright! Fuck it I'm out of here, and will go find
someone who could do it right!" Kandy-Cola
shouted and got out of the doggy style position
and off the bed, while pouting.

"Shut up! You know I hate when you talk
like that!" Roger shouted and grabs her by the
arm tightly.

"Roger get the hell off of me, your time
is up! You played with the pussy instead of
handling your business like a real man. I got
shit to do and money to chase!" Kandy-Cola
shouted.

FETISH

"Is that all you think about and care about is money?" Roger yelled.

"What the fuck else is there to care about. What? I should be a sucker for love like your punk ass!" Kandy Cola said sarcastically with a sick smirk on her face.

Roger's facial expression tightens up in anger as he grabs her by her hair.

"Ahhh!" She screams as he tosses her hard back onto the bed.

"What the fuck are you doing?" She screams as he forces her flat onto her stomach, then she felt her thick voluptuous butt cheeks being spread wide open.

She wiggles and squirms to get free of his grip. Then he holds open her ass cheeks and she stops moving as she felt his warm soft tongue, gently traveling from her clit to her pussy hole.

"Mmmm, shiit! No stop! What are you doing?" She moans in a lustful tone as the touch of his tongue excited her and sent a sweet teasing sensation through her body.

The sweet taste of her lingers in his mouth as he French kisses her clit while sucking on it, then let's the tip of his tongue flick up and down.

⬛Shiiit! Damn baby, fuck! That's what I'm talking about, handle your business.⬜ She moans while making a hissing sound.

Roger's tongue slowly inches its way to her anus. He licks around it in a circular motion.

⬛Mmmm!⬜ He moans with her as he inserts his tongue deep into her asshole.

⬛Ohhh! Ohhh! Ooowee!⬜She moans as his tongue went in and out of her asshole while he played with her clit hen sticks two fingers inside her wet pussy.

The mixture of sensations drove her into ecstasy as she climaxes onto his fingers.

⬛Damn baby, fuck me! Fuck me!⬜She screamed.

Roger pulls his fingers out of her wet-box and tongue out her ass. He uses the back of his forearm to wipe her sweet juices from his mouth and chin. He spits onto the palm of his hand and rubs it on the tip of his dick then climbs on top of her. Kandy-Cola winds her hips at the feeling of her body press against his. His hands spread her ass cheeks even wider as he slowly works his dick inside her ass.

⌈Mmmm! Shhh⌉ Shiiit! Yes! Yesss like that!⌉She moans as he works the head of his dick deeper inside her then pushes himself all the way deep inside her.

⌈Ahhh! Ahhh! Fuck yes!⌉She screams as he grinds his hips left to right then in a circular motion, while inside her teasing and pleasing her at the same time.

⌈Is this what you wanted?⌉Roger yelled while sticking two fingers in her opened mouth.

⌈Mmmm, yes! Yesss!⌉She moaned as he pounds deeper and harder with long strokes while still grinding from right to left.

He sticks his fingers more into her mouth and pulls her cheek to the side.

⌈Ahhh! Ahhh! Ahhh! Yes! I'm cumin! I'm fucking cumin!⌉ Kandy-Cola shouted as she climaxes twice.

Roger bit down on his bottom lip as he thrusts in and out of her even faster and harder.

FETISH

Ugghhh! He groans as he releases all his semen inside her asshole.

He pulls out and lay next to her out of breath, breathing hard with his body covered in sweat. He turns his head and looks at Kandy-Cola s beautiful face. She was what any man could ever dream of sexy, intelligent and great in bed.

I love you. He said meaning it then turns his head and closes his eyes.

He couldn t help but feel the vibration of her heart beating.

Give me a second and I ll be ready for round two. He mumbled then felt the weight of the bed shift.

Roger quickly opens his eyes and turns his head back over to see Kandy-Cola standing there stuffing her thong in her purse then wiggling back into her jeans and shirt.

Wait! Wait! What are you doing? I m not even done yet. Roger stated.

Kandy-Cola looks at him while raising her right eye brow and twists up her top lip to the side.

And whose problem is that, because it sure the hell isn't mines? I told you I got things to do and people to see. Kandy-Cola replied while sliding on her Jimmy Choo heels.

You mean you got people to do, mostly rappers and money you trying see. Roger spit back with an attitude.

See you men are all the same, you give a nigga an inch he wants to try and take a yard. Take it how you want to, I can care less, but get your ass up and dressed and take me back home to Far Rockaway. Kandy-Cola said while holding her hips and not caring how he was feeling for the moment.

'This fool thinks that just because he spent ten thousand dollars on me he can keep me here all day. I got bigger fish to catch and better shit to do with my time, then to spend it with someone with a credit card limit.' Kandy-Cola thought to herself and giggles out loud.

Oh you think this shit is funny, you came like three times and I only came once so I'm not taking you home! Roger shouted.

Hmm, do you really want to do this and play yourself? If you think you barely see me enough now what do you think is going to happen if you keep acting like a spoiled child? Man up, and don't act like a lame it's not your style boo, and it doesn't look good on you.⬜ Kandy-Cola said while twisting her head like a chicken head hood chick.

⬜Schmmp!⬜ Roger sucks his teeth and pops off the bed and gets dressed while frustrated, then stomps out the front door of his apartment with Kandy-Cola following behind him and laughs devilishly as she walks out his apartment building to his Hummer truck and gets in.

Chapter 5

Juicy sat in her sisters gray s430 Mercedes Benz, nervously wondering how her world got turned upside down.

⌐You need to stop acting so damn scared Juicy; it□s just a few dates not that big of a deal.□Tatiana said while pulling up to a large house in Greatneck Long Island.

You been trying to get me to do dates as long as I can remember, this shit isn□t for me Tatiana.□ Juicy stated while folding her arms with an attitude.

⌐Listen sister, you need to get with the program. You lost your damn job today from being late and a damn co-worker stole some money out the store in Rockefeller Center and your ass got the blame. You□re lucky you□re not locked up right now. Juicy we have bills and a mortgage to pay and food to buy and you□re the only one short on their share of money Juicy. So stop fucking complaining and let□s get this money. You will be just fine.□Tatiana said as she steps out the car and straightens the tight fitted dress she had on and fixes her fourteen inch weave then proceeds to walk to the front door of the large house.

Before she gets to the front door to ring the bell it opens up. A Caucasian man in his late 40's with blonde and gray hair stood there with a Kool-Aid smile on his face, behind him stood a woman with brunet hair. From the little lines by the corner of her eyes you could tell she was close to his age or older, she had on a tan strapless dress.

"Tatiana, come in. You did bring your friend right?" The man asked while continuing to grin.

"Yes she's in the car, she's just a little shy this is her first real date." Tatiana replied. J

Juicy puts her hands on her chest, her heart felt as if it wanted to break free and bust out of her chest from beating so hard and fast. She pulls out her phone from her pink Coach purse and called her best friend Marvin, who picks up on the first ring.

"What's good Juicy booty?" He said in his deep bass voice that seems to always travel through her body to her clit and gives her chills.

Juicy knew Marvin for seven years. He was a light skinned complexion with a slim built body and wore glasses, but yet a handsome man. She called him a hermit and a square dude that was into his books and had no bad boy thug side to him at all, unlike the men she and her friends were more attracted too. She had slept with him a few times but it was nothing serious to her, she valued their friendship more.

"Juicy are you okay, you haven't said nothing since you got on the phone, what's going on? You only really call when you're in trouble or want to talk my ear off. So which one is it?" Marvin asked.

"Shut up! Stop acting like you know me so well!" Juicy replied.

"But I do know you well. I bet you got pink on right now and your pink purse." Marvin said while laughing.

Juicy looks down at her chest at her pink dress she had on.

"Well that's not the point why I'm calling you. I'm petrified right now." Juicy replied.

"Why, what's going on?" Marvin asked.

"Well, Tatiana dragged me along on this date. I lost my job this morning and have no way to come up with my part of the mortgage.☐ Juicy replied.

Marvin stood quiet for a while before speaking then sighs.

☐You know she☐s been trying to get you to do dates with her for years. Juicy just say no and go home. You☐re not doing it. Your ass is a freak not a hoe.☐Marvin responded.

☐Juicy come on!☐Tatiana shouted from the front doorway of the house.

☐I have to go Marvin, I need the money and I just wanted to give you the address if anything should happen to me. I☐m in Greatneck Long Island I☐l text you the full address right now.☐Juicy replied and hung up the phone and steps out the car.

As she walks to the front door, where Tatiana was waiting, she text Marvin the house address.

☐Juicy this is Robert Miller and his wife Lynne.☐Tatiana said as Juicy steps further into the house.

Juicy looks at the overweight Caucasian man and his wife as they smile at her as if she was a meal they was about to devour.

"Ummm, you have a very nice home." Juicy said nervously while still looking around the house, to avoid eye contact with them.

"There's no reason to be shy." Robert said.

"Now come on and follow us." Lynne said as she leads Tatiana and Juicy upstairs.

Juicy studies everything as her heart races. She noticed the first room she passed was the master bedroom that the married couple slept in. Lynne opens a door on the left side of the hallway. The room was dark with a red dimmed light in the room. There were four chains on the far side of the wall and all kinds of sex toys on a small table. There were paddles that were different shapes and sizes, whips, dildos, strap-on dildos, nipple pickers and dick clamp.

"Okay, you go change while my wife and I get ready." Robert said and left the room with Lynne by his side.

"Change?" Juicy asked with a puzzled look on her face.

"Yes we have to change and get into our role. These two are into some weird things, whatever you do, don't fucking freak out, just go with the flow. They pay a lot of money to have their fetish satisfied. Tatiana said as she drops her purse in the corner of the room and wiggles out of her black dress.

Then she grabs an outfit that was hanging on a metal rack in the room. She passes it to Juicy, then grabs one for herself and slowly works her way into a full body, shiny, patent-leather body suit.

Zip me up Juicy booty. Tatiana said with her back turned, calling Juicy by her nickname she had given her.

Tatiana turns her head and could see that she was hesitating on doing anything. She hadn't even begun to change her clothes.

Juicy, snap out of it, this is for our mortgage money, to keep a roof over our heads. You better not fuck this up bitch. Now zip me up and change your clothes.

Juicy took a deep breath and zips up the back of Tatiana's patent-leather body suit then wiggles into her own outfit. Tatiana grabs a wooden paddle off the small table in the room and a long leather whip that she hands to Juicy as the Miller's enter the room and shuts the door. Juicy didn't know if she wanted to bust out laughing or if she should run pass them out the room.

Robert was on his hands and knees with a leather face mask on, that had a zipper over the mouth part. He had on a dog like color with spikes around his neck that was connected to a chrome metal chain in Lynne's hand. He was completely butt naked. The fat on his body hung out. The only thing that was slightly like clothing was a leather harness that ran across his chest and back. Mrs. Miller stood dressed in five inch red patent-leather heels with a tight matching red mini skirt, with a nipples bra. She also was wearing a black Brazilian hat on her head.

"Let's get started." Tatiana said as she walks over to the couple seductively.

She grabs the chain leash out of Lynne's hand and bends over and swung hard with all her might with the paddle in her hand.

"Ahhh! Ahhh!" Robert hollered in pain as the paddle smacked his bone cheek hard.

"Shut the fuck up!" Tatiana shouted then slaps him on the ass once more with the paddle.

FETISH

⌐Ahhh! Ahhh!⌐ Robert screams once more as his pale white butt cheeks turn red.

⌐Now get up!⌐Tatiana ordered.

He stood up as he was ordered to do and Tatiana leads him to the wall and cuffs his hands to it, with his back facing her. Juicy stood there speechless in shock, not knowing what the hell was going on.

⌐Juicy, what in the fuck are you doing? Bring that bitch over here and cuff her to the fucking wall!⌐Tatiana shouted in a demanding tone.

⌐Come with me to the wall Mrs. Miller.⌐ Juicy said in a sweet voice that sounded innocent and childlike.

Tatiana⌐s facial expression twisted up in disbelief. She stomps over to Juicy and Lynne.

⌐You don⌐t talk to her like that! You have to treat this bitch like the shit piece of hoe she is! Like this!⌐Tatiana shouted then slaps fire out of Lynne.

⌐Ahhh! Ahhh!⌐She screams in pain as her head twists from the blow.

She then turns her head back and rubs her face then licks her lips in lust.

Now you smack her and then beat her with that whip in your hands on her back, ass and thighs. Try not to leave any marks on her face that can be noticed. Tatiana said.

Smack her, are you sure? Juicy asks nervously.

Tatiana tilts her head sideways and twists up her lips giving Juicy a look that read, bitch you better smack this woman before I knock your ass out. Juicy knew her sister all too well and could read her facial expression.

'Damn what have I gotten myself into? Tatiana is going to be pissed off at me if I mess this up. We need the mortgage money.' Juicy thought to herself then pulls her arm back and slaps Lynen lightly on the face.

Harder! Lynne screamed.

Juicy could feel Tatiana's eyes staring at her and felt them burning into her skull. Anger came over Juicy as she smacks Lynne twice with all her might.

Ahhh! Ahhh! Lynne cried out in pain.

"That's right! Teach that cunt a lesson!" Tatiana shouted with a smile on her face as Juicy starts beating Lynne with the horse whip on her thigh.

"Ahhhhh! Ahhhhh! Yes! I love it!" Lynne screams in pleasure and pain.

"Get your ass over to the fucking wall!" Juicy shouted, doing her best to act like her big sister.

While Lynne walks Juicy continues to whip her on the back and thighs until she was against the wall and then she cuffs her hands chaining her to it.

"You both have been very bad and we're going to punish you real good!" Tatiana shouted then looks at Juicy giving her the signal to continue beating Lynne.

With each blow to Mrs. and Mr. Miller's back and ass from the paddle and whip their bodies went into ecstasy. The pain brought a great joy and teasing sensation like no other.

"You fucking like that that, don't you?" Tatiana shouted.

"Yes." Mr. Robert hollered as his dick got harder and he came on the wall.

Their fucking enjoying this too much but I got something for them. Tatiana said as she walks back over to the small round table filled with different kinds of sex toys.

She grabs two pairs of nipple pickers, then two strap-on nine inch thick dildos and walks back over and passed one to Juicy.

What am I supposed to with this? Juicy asks with a confused look on her face.

Tatiana stares at her with a look that said bitch you cant be that stupid.

Fuck that cunt! Tatiana shouted as she digs in her purse that was resting on the floor in the corner of the room and pulls out a bottle of KY hot and sweet jelly.

She tightens the strap on around her pelvis area and lubes up the nine inch black dildo. Then she spreads Roberts butt cheeks and inserts the tip of the dildo inside his rectum. She works it in and out.

Ugghhh! Robert groans in joy as Tatiana went deeper and deeper.

He arches his back while holding the wall that he was handcuffed to. Tatiana reaches her hand around his fat shaking stomach and grabs his four inch hard pink dick. She jerks it off as she thrusts in and out of his asshole.

Ohhh! Ahhh!! Yesss! I♭e been so bad! Robert screamed as a tear ran down the side of his face.

'What in the hell did I step into?' Juicy asks herself as she watched Tatiana dick down Mr. Miller as if she was a man.

I might as well follow her lead. Juicy said out loud as she turns her head to see Mrs. Miller sticking her old wrinkle pile ass up in the air with her palms flat on the wall.

Juicy shook her head in disgust and ties the strap-on dildo around her pelvis area then walks over next to Tatiana and picks up the bottle of KY-Jelly that was on the floor. She lubes up the thick dildo then walks back over to Mrs. Miller and grabs her waist and slowly inserts the dildo inside her vagina. Juicy tries to hide the feeling of disgust on her face.

Harder! Harder! I♭e been bad! Mrs. Miller shouted.

Juicy♭s facial expression tightens as anger builds up inside her body as she thrusts in and out of Mrs. Miller like a mad woman, while smacking her on her thighs and ass cheeks.

"Yes! Yes! Oh my God yes! I'm cumin!" Mrs. Miller hollered as her body went into a convulsion and starts to shake as she climaxes.

Two hours later Tatiana and Juicy had fucked the Millers in every sexual position they could think of with the strap-on dildos.

They sat in Tatiana's grey Mercedes Benz counting their money while still sitting in front of the house.

"See bitch didn't I tell you that it would be easy. Look for two hours of work we made $1,500 apiece, and two hundred dollars tip." Tatiana stated then puts her money in her purse.

"Yea, but that was some crazy shit, on some S&M mess. I never knew people could really like things like that and an older white couple at that." Juicy replied.

"Trick please, most of my dates are Caucasian people. They spend the most money and are into fetish and S&M, but all the dates we have won't be that easy and some will be freakier. Tatiana said as she started up the car.

So we're going home now, right? Juicy asks in a childlike manner.

Bitch please we're just getting started the day and night is still young. Tatiana replied as she pulls off.

Why? We made more than enough money for our cut of the mortgage, we got seventeen hundred apiece. I don't get paid this much in three weeks. Juicy replied.

There's way more money to make and we're going to get it all. What's in our purses is chump change to me. Tatiana said as she stops at a red light and picks up a half smoked blunt of weed in her ashtray and sparks it up.

She took a few pulls and inhales deeply and looks at Juicy in her pink dress and gets turned on as she stares at her thick thighs. She leans over and pulls Juicy's face towards her and softly and deeply kisses her lips. Their tongues danced in each other's mouths as Juicy lets out a slight moan.

Beep! Beep! The sound of a loud horn could be heard coming from the car behind them, broke their embrace.

Shut the fuck up! Tatiana stuck her head out the driver's side window and shouted, then looks up to see that the light had turned green. She steps on the accelerator and pulls off.

Chapter 6

Across the street parked in a green 2002 Lincoln was a man watching Tatiana and Juicy pull off. He had been sitting in the car stalking them for two hours. Rage and anger consumed his body and showed on his face as his imagination played tricks on him and he pictures what kind of freaky things Juicy and Tatiana had done in the Millers house. He steps out the car and looks both ways making sure none of the neighbors was outside or looking out their windows as he made his way to the huge house. He raises his hand to knocks on the front door, but something told him to twist the door knob instead. A wicked grin spread across his face, when the front door opens right up.

'Damn crazy ass white people never believe in locking their doors. Always feeling so safe in their upper class neighborhood, but always wants someone from my hood to take care of their sexual needs.' The man said out loud to his self as he steps into the house then shuts the door behind himself.

The house was completely silent except from the loud moaning and smacking sounds, that was coming from upstairs, his hand touched the smooth cherry wood rail that he guessed cost a fortune, as he slowly creeps up the stairs and continues to follow the sound of moaning and smacking, to reach a door down the hallway on the left with a dim red light shining through the crack of the door. He cautiously pushes open the door and couldn't believe his eyes. Mr. Miller was bent over on the floor with a black leather sex mask on his face that had a zipper on the mouth area, the zipper was wide open, leaving Mr. Miller's pink lips poking out as he hollered and screamed in ecstasy. Around his neck was a dog collar with metal spikes on it. Connected to his balls and dick and nipples were long chrome thin wires that lead to some kind of device in Mrs. Miller's hands. Every time she pressed the little green button that sent 500 electric volts through the wires that were attached to Mr. Miller's body.

Ahhhh! Ahhhh! Shit, fuck yes! I've been bad, so bad! Mr. Miller hollered.

Mrs. Lynne smacks him on his old sagging wrinkled ass that was now bright red with paddle marks. She presses the button repeatedly while beating him silly with the paddle.

FETISH

"Ahhhh! Ahhhh! I've been bad!" He screams as he urinates on the wooden floor.

"Yes you've been a bad dog!"Mrs. Miller shouted.

The man at the doorway had seen more than enough. He pulls out a yellow box cutter then pushes the razor blade up. Then he opens the door wider and walks in sneaking up on Mrs. and Mr. Miller. He accidently steps on a bottle of KY-Jelly that let out a loud squirting sound as it splashes onto the floor. Mrs. Miller turns around and sees the intruder and screams.

"Ahhhh! Ahhhh!"Her screams and cries were cut short by the man as he runs toward her taking her to the ground knocking the air out of her lungs.

Mr. Miller was still in the doggy style position. When he turned his head and sees his wife knocked down on the floor and a brown skinned man on top of her repeatedly punching her in the face.

"Ahhhh! Ahhhh!"Mrs. Miller screamed at the top of her lungs when she caught her breath.

⌐Uggaa!⌐ She then made a gagging sound as the razor from the box cutter went across her neck three times splitting it open.

⌐Uggaa!⌐She gasps for air then tries to hold her neck as blood gushes out and pours onto the floor like a running water hose.

⌐Lynne!⌐Mr. Miller shouted.

Before he could get up straight to stand up, the brown skin man jumps off of Mrs. Miller and ran over and kicks Mr. Miller in the ribs as if he was kicking a football into a field goal.

⌐Uggaa!⌐ Mr. Miller grunted in pain as his fat stomach jiggles and he rolls over to the side on the floor.

The brown skinned man scans the room real quick and sees all the sex toys on a table on the far side of the room. He ran over to the table and grabs the long wooden paddle that was covered in black leather that had tiny metal spikes on it.

⌐Damn, you people are sick!⌐ He said as he took a practice swing with the paddle then he looks at Mrs. Miller to see that she was still alive, her body was still going into convulsions as it buckle and shake up and down like a wet fish out of water. Somehow she had managed to slow down the blood from pouring out of her neck by wrapping both her hands tightly around the open wounds. The man looks back at Mr. Miller wobbling around groaning in pain on the floor.

Ahhhh! Ohhhh! Uggaa! he grunted.

The Stalker raises the wooden paddle that was covered in leather with tiny metal spikes on it and came down with all his might repeatedly on his chest and stomach then thighs.

Ahhhh! Ahhhh! Mr. Miller hollered in pain as the tiny metal spikes on the paddle rips into his skin, opening up little holes all over Mr. Miller s body.

Stop! Please stop! No! Ahhhh! Ahhhh! Ahhhh! He screams as the paddle crashes into his face, then chest.

The small metal spikes got stuck in the fat on Mr. Miller s stomach. The Stalker tries to pull it out but couldn t He yanks as hard as he could making the spikes that was stuck in Mr. Miller s stomach rip away a larger chunk of flesh.

FETISH

⌈Ahhhh! Ahhhh! Ahhhh! Ahhhh! No! Why are you doing this to us?⌋Mr. Miller cried out in a weak voice as the paddle came crashing down on his nose, breaking it and then comes down on his dick.

⌈You⌋re fucking freaks!⌋ The Stalker shouted then gains his composure as he realizes he was now covered in blood and Mr. Miller was barely moving.

Mrs. Miller⌋s body was still flopping around like a fish as she held her neck with her eyes wide open watching the brutal assault of her husband in horror. The Stalker looks at the dying couple one more time then bends down and unzips the leather sex mask on Mr. Miller and removes it from his face then took off the dog collar off his neck.

⌈Noooo, please no more! Call the ambulance, save my wife please.⌋Mr. Miller begged as he coughs up blood.

All his ribs were cracked and the tiny metal spikes on the paddle had ripped tiny holes through his whole body and tore chunks of flesh of his stomach and arms leaking blood everywhere. The Stalker walks out of the room and down the hallway and found a bathroom.

He walks to the sink and turns on the cold water.

'What the fuck have I done? Why did I do this?' The Stalker said out loud to himself as he splashes cold water on his face.

'I did it for them.' He said out loud then looks at the leather sex mask in his hand along with the dog collar with spikes on it.

Inside of the mask it was covered with thick red sticky blood from when he was beating Mr. Miller in the face with the paddle. The cold water sent chills through the Stalker's body as he held the mask under the running water rinsing away the blood. He then wipes it on his jeans drying it off. He stares at the mask for a moment then slowly puts it on, zipping the back of it shut, making it lock onto his face. The Stalker stares at his self in the mirror, slightly leaning his neck from side to side.

'Hmmm I'm missing something.' He said out loud to himself then ties the dog collar with the spikes around his neck then zips close the zipper on the mouth piece on the leather sex mask. *'Perfect.'* He thought to himself as his eyes open up wide like a maniac, crazy dope fiend bum you would see on the streets.

FETISH

⌐Agghhh! Ahhhh! Ugghhh!⌐ Moaning sounds snap him out his trance.

He stops looking at himself in the mirror and walks back down the hallway to the sex room. To his surprise the Millers were very much still alive and moving around.

⌐You fucking weirdos like pain huh?⌐ The Stalker shouted as he picks the small electric Taser that was connected to Mr. Millers body parts through wires, until the Stalker beat the clip off that was connected to him.

The Stalker unzips his zipper and pulls out his dick.

⌐Mmmm!⌐ He moaned as a stream of pee came flowing out of him and onto the Millers who looked at him with terror in their eyes.

The Stalker puts his dick away and zips up his zipper then turns the volts on the electric Taser to high and spreads the wires connected to it out on their bodies.

⌐You two are fucking weird. Do you know what happens when you mix any wet fluids with electricity? No, I'll show you." The Stalker said and pushes the green button.

"Noooo! Ahhhh!" Mrs. Miller screamed the best she could, and lets go of her neck, letting the blood from the wound in her neck flow out as her body flops up and down.

She turns her head and looks at her husband before her eye's popped out of her eye sockets, then burst like grapes being stepped on.

"Noooo! Lynne!" Mr. Miller shouted as white foam came out the side of his mouth and the image of his eye balls exploding played over and over in his head as the 500 volts travel through his body.

"See your ass is fat, it's going take longer for you to die. Die you little fat piggy." The Stalker said then sniffs the air.

'It smells like bacon or burnt chicken.' The Stalker said out loud to his self then turns up the voltage on the Taser.

"Ahhhh! Ahhhh! Ughhhaa!" Mr. Miller hollered as his skin cooks and bubbles up turning bright red and black as white form and puss comes out his eyes and mouth when he finally stop moving.

The Stalker smiled, but it couldnⓣ be seen because the leather sex masks mouth piece was zipped closed. The Stalker left the room and house satisfied of what he had done, taking the electric Taser, the eighteen inch paddle covered in tiny spikes and hops into his car and pulls off.

Chapter 7

'Damn I really don't have time to get too much done because of Roger's slow ass trying to keep me even longer. I have real money to get, that little bit of credit card money he dished out wasn't nothing but crumbs to a boss bitch like me.' Kandy-Cola said out loud to herself as she ran the hot water in the bathroom sink and places her green wash cloth under it.

'I don't even have the time to take a shower. I guess a bird bath will have to do or a whore bath like my mother would call it. Hahahahaha!' Kandy☐Cola said and bust out laughing at her own joke then stops when she heard the new song, 'Let Me See Your Ass Clap', by Casino☐Rich and Goonz Squad playing from the small digital radio that was on top of the bathroom mirror.

She turns up the song then soaps up the washcloth and ran it across her vagina and ass, washing it the best she could while dancing.

'Don't worry I'm going to make that ass clap for you real soon baby. She said as if she was talking to Casino-Rich through the radio.

She finishes up her bird bath then pulls her Mac makeup kit from inside the medicine cabinet on the wall. Her hand moves smoothly as she applies her eye shadow, then her blush and then some red lipstick. She quickly runs to her bedroom down the stairs on the first floor naked and sees Shanelle on the couch eating chips while watching music videos.

Where is your hooking ass going in such a rush? Shanelle said while turning around on the couch looking at Kandy-Cola's perfect thickly shaped body as she runs by.

Kandy-Cola stops for a brief second and looks at Shanelle and shook her head.

'I love that skinny bitch, but she really needs to step her hustle game up. That abortion scam isn't always going to cut it and it's no real money anyway.' Kandy-Cola thought to herself.

I'm going on a date with Casino Rich then later to Club Imperial with him and his team. Kandy-Cola said bragging.

Word, I just got done watching his new video with them sexy ass goon squad niggas. Can I roll with you? Shanelle replied.

Schmmp! Kandy-Cola sucks her teeth.

'Shanelle's a bad bitch but her little fat pregnant belly will fuck up my flow up and have Casino-Rich looking at me funny, like this is the type of chicks you hang with. That bitch is going to drop my stock value and right now my stock is to damn high. There isn't a chick that has shit on me in this game.' Kandy-Cola thought to herself.

Ummm, don't you think your stomach is a little too big to be going clubbing. I don't think they would even let you in, in your condition. Kandy-Cola said with a sneaky smirk on her face.

What, I'm only two months and besides I'm heading to the chop shop and get an abortion tomorrow morning anyways. Shanelle said defensively then stood up off the couch looking at Kandy-Cola.

Your skinny Shanelle, so you show a lot for two months. It looks as if you're four months pregnant. Listen I don't have time for this girl, I got moves to make. Kandy-Cola said as she turns around and heads for her room.

Whatever bitch, you always think you're better than everybody else because of your damn body. I'll like to see what you're going to do when that shit fades and gets fat and sloppy! Shanelle shouted with her hands on her hips.

Yeah, yeah, I love you too heifer you can roll with me next time. Kandy-Cola shouted from her room and shuts the door.

Her motive for not wanting Shanelle to come with her was a complete lie. The truth was that she had only met Casino-Rich once at Club Perfections. They exchanged numbers and talked. Casino-Rich already knew who she was, her name rang bells as one bad ass women in New York City, and that she only dealt with real ballers, rappers, singers and producers. She had made her way half way through the music entertainment industry and they all had love for her but no one could seem to be able to lock her down and wife her. She would pull away when any of her relationships got to serious. The only one that was consistent in her life that she lets stay around for years was Roger. Even knowing he was a hermit in her eyes, just a regular working man, but he was loyal.

Kandy-Cola knew even though Shanelle was pregnant and slim, she gave off a natural sex appeal that put men and women into a trance and having a sexual relationship with her would blow any persons mind away. She knew how to work those big juicy lips of her.

'I can't have that bitch around slowing up my flow, there's already going to be enough groupies in the club. I have to put it on Casino and make him pussy whipped before I bring my girls around.' Kandy-Cola said out loud to herself as she works her thick voluptuous Coca Cola bottle shape body into a red Louis Vuitton skin tight fitted dress then slips her feet in the four inch new Christian Louboutin, Red Bottom shoes she had used Roger's credit card to buy earlier in the day. Last but not least, she grabs her black small purse.

Shanelle watches Kandy-Cola walk right passed her in the living room and out the front door. Shanelle got off the couch and walks to the living room window and peeps through the curtains and watches Kandy-Cola's white Range Rover start up and pull off the block.

'That bitch swears she's the shit, but I'm going, but to switch my hustle and get on the same shit she be on, Kandy isn't the only one that can pull a rapper or a singer.' Shanelle

thought to herself as she pulls out her iPhone and made a call.

"Hello I need a cab at 224 Beach 60th Street. I'm going to Brooklyn." Shanelle said then hung up the phone.

Casino-Rich's mansion had eight bedrooms and five bathrooms. It was a huge house in Port Washington, Long Island, New York by the ocean. It was just one of the many homes he owned.

Casino-Rich was a fast up and coming rapper and just like his name was growing, so was his bank account. He was on every mixed tape, and if he wasn't every artist wanted him on their remix.

With his long dreaded hair and brown skinned complexion that was tatted up all over his body and catchy hooks on his songs, it wasn't hard to tell why women loved him and his style. But the only woman on his mind was the famous Kandy-Cola.

He took another pull of his blunt filled with sour diesel weed. He pulls back on the pool stick and hits the number seven ball into the left corner pocket of the red pool table.

FETISH

"I just can't read her." Casino-Rich said out loud.

"That was random, who are you talking about?" His right hand man and leader of the Goonz Squad Alonzo asked.

"Kandy-Cola, I can't figure that chick out. Since the first night I met her, like she didn't know or care who the fuck I am." Casino-Rich replied while waiting for Alonzo to take his shot and stood there dazed thinking about Kandy-Cola.

"Man fuck that stuck up bitch, we got pussy walking all through this house." Alonzo said as he smacks the ass of a young Spanish woman wearing only a white thong and matching bra standing next to the pool table drinking Champagne and smoking a blunt.

"We got chains on our necks that cost more than people's homes a fleet of luxury cars and houses in different states. Why in the fuck are you worrying about Kandy-Cola? That bitch just has a banging body, that's all." Alonzo responded as three more sexy women walk into the game room only wearing panties and bras.

FETISH

The brown skinned one licks her lips and stared seductively at Casino-Rich. He looks at her turns his head and went back to playing pool.

"Yo, you bitches go somewhere else. I'm trying to have a conversation with my man. There's plenty of Goonz Squad rich niggas that would love to dick you down. So go and find one or two!" Casino-Rich shouted as he took his shot and misses the yellow number two pool ball.

"Damn, pass me that blunt homie." He ordered Alonzo.

He took three pulls of the blunt packed with diesel weed. "Kandy-Cola is the one bad Bitch in New York. I have to grab her up. She only fucks with niggas getting that real paper and no one in the industry has been able to lock her down and wife her, but I will. Just watch and see." Casino-Rich said.

"Schmmp!" "Nigga you sound high, dumb or soft. Why in the hell would you want to wife that bitch that dealt with 40% of the entertainment industry?" Alonzo stated.

Casino-Rich drops his pool stick and walks over to Alonzo and slaps him three times in the blink of an eye. Alonzo backpedals with his facial expression balled up in anger and with his fist tightened and ready to swing. Casino-Rich pulls out the Glock 9mm that was on is waist and aims it at Alonzo's forehead stopping him dead in his tracks. Alonzo froze just standing there with his hands up.

Yea nigga go ahead and flex if you want. I'll lay you where you stand! Casino-Rich shouted.

The Spanish woman that was still in the room only wearing a thong and bra screams as she stares at the gun in Casino-Rich's hand.

Ahhhh!

Bitch shut up, and go in another room! Casino-Rich shouted. The woman quickly made her way out of the room with tears running down her face.

Alonzo tries to control his anger as he stared at Casino-Rich.

Damn this nigga just slapped me and punks me like a bitch.' Alonzo thought to himself as his pride ate away at him.

A small voice in his head told him to reach for his own gun on his waist, but he knew better, unlike most rappers that fake like their gangsters and thugs. Casino-Rich and the 37 members of the Goonz Squad was the real thing. They started off in their hometown in Houston, Texas selling weight of bricks of cocaine and murdered many people along the way to the top. Then they invested the money into their rap company Goonz Squad Hustlers, with Casino-Rich's catchy hooks and thug swag, they quickly got signed with Interscope Records in a month, breaking a deal worth millions and blows up in the rap scene.

Alonzo was far from weak or a punk being that he was Casino-Rich's right hand man and best friend, but wasn't any fool and had seen Casino-Rich kill over less disrespect.

Alright! Alright! Just chill nigga, you know I didn't mean anything by it. I love you like a brother. Alonzo said copping the plea with both hands up.

I love you like a brother too but I will kill your ass where you stand and won't think twice about it, don't ever bite the hand that feed you. You're supposed to kill any dog that do and watch your mouth next time. Casino-Rich said as he lowers his gun and puts it back on his waist then gives Alonzo a dap and a hug.

Alonzo smiled but on the inside was burning up with rage. They broke their embrace as Casino-Rich's personal bodyguard, D-Wes enters the room.

D-Wes was three hundred pounds of muscle with a fat gut, a massive of a man. He was dressed in all black a tight t-shirt with black jeans with gun holsters around his shoulders. On his neck was a platinum Goonz Squad medallion.

"Why are you two hugging like little girls and shit?" D-Wes said in his deep Barry White voice.

"Shut the hell up!" Alonzo shouted.

"Yeah, yeah, but anyway, there's a young lady here that wants to see the boss." D-Wes replied.

"Man I don't want to see none of those hoes, send her to one of the other rooms and let her groupie ass jump off with one of the other homies." Casino-Rich responded.

"Oh I have a feeling you want to see this one Boss." D-Wes said with a huge grin on his face as he steps his massive body to the side and Kandy-Cola walks in wearing an all red

Louis Vuitton dress with the matching shoes that hugged every curve on her body.

Casino-Rich and Alonzo along with D Wes stared at her with their mouths open wide and lust in their eyes undressing her in their minds. Kandy-Cola had the most perfect body on a woman they ever laid eyes on, the shape of a goddess. Her waist line was slim with no fat on her stomach. Her hips and thighs poked out and her ass was voluptuous and perfect. The kind you would only see on a stripper and she had the perfect size double CC breast that set up nice and perky. She had a face of an angel with juicy luscious lips and light brown eyes that you can get lost in.

So you were just going to send me away like one of those groupies? Kandy-Cola said with her hands on her hips standing there as if she was posing for a photo shoot.

Casino-Rich stood there lost for words while still staring.

I guess I ll go then because I m far from being one of these hoes or being treated like one of these groupie bitches. Kandy-Cola said as she spins around on her heels and starts walking, while her heels hit the brown hard wood floor her ass cheeks switch from left to right looking like two juicy soft basketballs.

No baby, hold up! I didnt know it was you. Casino-Rich said firmly finally speaking for the first time after snapping out of his daze of lust.

Kandy-Cola kept walking right passed DWes and out the room and down the hallway. There was nothing she loved more than playing mind games with a man of power and making them work for it.

DWes and Alonzo watched Casino-Rich chase after her, something he never did, but they both could understand why.

Damn I must have been drunk in the club when we meet her shes the baddest bitch Ive ever seen in my damn life. Alonzo thought to himself.

Kandy, wait a minute, please! Casino-Rich said while grabbing her arm.

Kandy-Cola stops with her back turned to him and folded her arms.

Why should I stop? Youre not about to be disrespecting me or think you can treat me like one of your fucking groupies. Your ass is about to have a rude awakening if you think so!▯She shouted.

▯Naw baby, I didn▯t know it was you. I thought it was one of those bitches running around here. I want nothing to do with them so I send them to mess with my team. You been the only woman stuck in my mind since I met you in the club the other night.▯ Casino-Rich said as he turns her around to face him.

▯Damn go down! Go down!▯He said to himself in his mind as he felt his dick becoming aroused growing and wanted to break free from his jeans as he stares at her face and his met her.

'Damn this nigga sexy with his long dreads and look at all the jewelry he has on. He's feeding into my trap I got him wrapped around my finger already. It's a matter of time before I'll be milking him for everything I want.' Kandy-Cola thought to herself.

▯You▯re just trying to game me, I told you I was going to come over today so we can chill.▯ Kandy-Cola said while twisting up her facial expression.

Casino-Rich couldn▯t help but to find her attractive.

FETISH

"To keep it real with you Kandy, after you turned me down from not coming home with me the other night, I didn't really think you would show up today, I gave you my number and address, you didn't text or call sweetie. Come here and let me make it up to you baby." Casino-Rich said with a Kool-Aid smile on his face.

Kandy-Cola couldn't help but to smile back.

"And how are you going to do that, if I may ask?" Kandy-Cola replied as Casino-Rich took her hand and lead her down the long hallway and up a spiral staircase.

Music could be heard blasting and moans of different type of women could be heard from a few of the bedrooms they passed.

"Do you always have your entourage stay with you?" Kandy-Cola asked sarcastically.

"No, but I like to keep them close just in case something pops off, besides this house is really for them. I have a condo in Manhattan just for me that we will go to next time. So I won't have my sexy wifey around these dudes." Casino-Rich stated as they enter the west wing of the mansion that was much quieter.

They stop at a large double door with gold trims on it and had the Goonz Squad logo of a pink diamond engraved on the door. He pushes open the room door and they enter the room. Kandy-Cola's jaw drops. She had been around a lot of celebrities and was hard to impress, but had to admit to herself that she was impressed.

The master bedroom was the size of most people apartments, and had a Jacuzzi hot tube in the middle of the room floor. Every trim on the walls and California King sized bed was made of 24 carat gold. Casino-Rich releases her hand and shuts the double doors behind them.

Ummm it just hit my brain, what do you mean your wifey or boo? When did I sign up for that job or title? Kandy-Cola asked while holding her hips.

See, that's what I like about you, any other woman will jump on the opportunity to be my woman or boo, but not you. Casino-Rich replied.

FETISH

"Well I'm not just any woman and no one has been able to wife me because I haven't let them. What makes you think you're any different?" Kandy-Cola replied.

"Because those dudes were weak, I'm a much stronger breed of a man and they was giving you chump change and act as if they was giving you the world. But I'm going to give you 50,000 every month and shower you with gifts that your heart desires." Casino-Rich said as he walks to a white dresser with gold trim on it and opens a draw and pulls out a checkbook.

"So what, I went from you treating me like a groupie bitch to now a prostitute?" Kandy-Cola said with her left eyebrow raised.

"No baby, you're no prostitute, I don't even look at you like that, but let's face it, you don't deal with no broke niggas and I'm far from being broke and pussy cost to maintain. I'm just trying to maintain you baby. Do you feel me?" Casino Rich said as he walks over to her and opens the palm of his left hand to reveal a check for 50,000 in her name and a choke collar platinum chain with the Goonz Squad logo eagle with pink diamonds incrusted in it.

FETISH

⬚So are you in or out.⬚ Casino-Rich stated.

Kandy-Cola looks down into his hands and act as if she really needed to think about, but smiles inside.

⬚I'm all in.⬚She replied while taking the check and putting it in her black small Louis Vuitton hand purse.

Casino-Rich grins from ear to ear as he puts the platinum choke collar chain around her neck.

⬚This means your mine and only mine. I will announce it tonight at Club Imperial, the radio stations will be there.⬚Casino-Rich said proud of himself to be the first and only man to lock down the famous Kandy-Cola.

Kandy-Cola licks her lips seductively, while unzipping the back of her red dress and lets it drop to her ankles and steps out of it. Casino-Rich stood there stuck for the second time for that day. Her body looks even better with no clothes on and the fact she hadn⬚worn any panties or bra turned him on even more, her double ⬚CC⬚breast sat up perfect without a bra. Tattoos of paw prints ran down the right side of her tight, thick voluptuous body, screaming fuck me. She had the word Sex Goddess tatted under her stomach close to her pelvic area.

Damn! How you got all those thighs and ass with no stomach? Casino-Rich asks while shaking his head and couldn't believe his eyes.

I work out a lot, so are you going to just stand there looking at me or are you going come over here and fuck the shit out of me with my Red Bottom heels on? Kandy-Cola asked seductively.

Casino-Rich wastes no time to work out of his jeans and boxers, setting free his eight inch dick then removes his shirt and tank top. Kandy-Cola looks at his chest, his stomach and arms all cover in tattoos and got moist immediately. She walks over to him seductively and drops to her knees.

Since you treat me right I'm going to treat you right. She said as she wraps her juicy lips around the head of his dark brown dick and lets her tongue flick up and down on it.

▯Mmmm, damn shorty.▯He moaned as his dick grew another inch from the warm wet sweet feeling of her mouth.

He looks down at her as she works her magic deep throating his dick without choking and playing with his balls with her left hand. Gagging sounds mixed with her soft moans echo throughout the room.

▯Damn baby!▯Casino-Rich groans as he held the back of her head.

Spit drips out her mouth and down to his balls then to the floor. She works her head back and forth while twisting her head from side to side.

▯Damn, fuck!▯Casino-Rich shouted with his eyes opened in disbelief.

'Out of all the women I've been with, no one has ever sucked my dick as good as this bitch is doing.' Casino-Rich thought to his self then felt himself about to explode.

Kandy-Cola sucked the tip of his dick then deep throat it and stops.

▯Wait why did you stop? I was just about to cum.▯ Casino-Rich said through clenched teeth frustrated.

I know and I don't want you to waste any of that sweet cum yet. She replied as she stood up straight and her high heels click on the hard wood floor.

He watches her fat plump ass switch from side to side as she walks to the California King sized bed and bends over on it. She looks back at him while wiggling her ass up and down.

Come over here and fuck the shit out of me. She moaned.

Casino-Rich wasted no time he was at the bed behind her in two large steps. He grips her ass cheeks and spread them as he slowly works his way inside her moist wet pussy.

Oh God your so fucking tight! I love it! He groaned as he gave her long deep slow strokes.

Choke me! Ayeee! Ohhh! Mmmm! She screamed.

His hand reaches around her neck and grips it and squeezes tightly, while picking up his pace.

FETISH

"Ugghhaa!" He groaned as he thrusts in and out of her while watching her perfect fat voluptuous ass shake. He smacks it.

"Yesss! Oooweee! Oh God yes! Fuck me! I love it!" Kandy-Cola moans as she throws her ass back at him.

"I want you to fuck me in my ass." She said in a slutty tone causing Casino-Rich to stop thrusting in and out of her as his facial expression twists up in disgust.

She turns her head and looks back at him and seen his face all balled up.

"Come on don't tell me you're one of those fake ass men who don't believe in anal sex." She stated.

"No I'm not, I'm just not in to anal sex I think it's nasty and I've never done it before. My dick doesn't belong in anyone's asshole, that shit's gay." Casino-Rich responded.

"Ugghhh, you sound like one of those slow ass niggas. How you don't know you won't like it, if you don't try it." Kandy-Cola replied.

"It's nasty, I'm not with it and I think its gay, plus I don't want shit all over my dick."

Casino-Rich responded with his facial expression still twisted up.

⬜You sound mad. You sound mad young and immature, I have needs, you said your my man now so it⬜s your job to for fill them all and if you don⬜t do it, I will find someone who will and won⬜t mind sticking their dick in this fat ass and isn⬜t scared to get a little shit on their dick.⬜ She said sarcastically then lays flat on the bed on her stomach and bounces her voluptuous ass, while sliding off her Red Bottom shoes.

'This bitch is trying to come at my manhood and then taking about giving my body away. Oh hell no she belongs to me.' Casino-Rich thought to himself as he climbs on top of her.

⬜What are you doing? Kandy-Cola said and knew her manipulating skills had worked. ⬜I told you there⬜s no need too I⬜ll find somebody else to do it.⬜

⬜Ahhh! Damn! Shhiiit!⬜Her words were cut short as she felt the head of his dick working its way into her ass.

⬜Damn, yes baby!⬜She moaned as she bites down into the pillow as he gave her long deep slow strokes, while holding his body up with the palm of his hands as if he was doing pushups.

"You're not going to give my body away! You belong to me now! Do you hear me?" Casino-Rich shouted through clenched teeth as he pounds in and out of her ass like a mad man.

"Ayee! Yesss! Ahhh! I hear you daddy, I belong to you! Damn you're fucking me so good!" She screamed.

"You better act like you know." He said as he pulls out his dick, then man handles her, flipping her around on to her back and push her legs up to her breast.

"I want to see your beautiful fucking face." He said as he spits on the palm of his left hand and rubs it on to the tip of his penis while jerking it back and forth.

He eases himself down and works himself back into her rectum.

"Oh God yesss! Mmmm! Ahhh! Ahhh!" Kandy-Cola screams and moans with each thrust as they stared into each other's eyes.

"That's right your mines now Kandy, you're my woman!" Casino-Rich's words were cut short as he stops talking when he felt Kandy-Cola hands spread his tight ass cheeks and stick the tip of her index finger into his anal.

"What the fuck are you doing? Get your finger out my fucking ass before I knock you out!"Casino-Rich shouted and looks at her as if he was ready to rip her head off.

"Stop it! I told you have needs and you have to fulfill them. Just go with the flow then tell me if you don't like it baby."She said while kissing his neck and chest seducing him.

Their lips met and they kiss deeply and passionately, their tongues dance around in each other's mouths. He slowly starts to grind his hips moving his dick all around inside her ass.

"Ahhh! Mmmm!"She moans while their lips were still locked in a deep kiss.

His facial expression balls up in pain as her index finger went deeper into his rectum. Soon Kandy-Cola's finger was going in and out of his ass with ease, just as fast as he was thrusting in and out of her.

"Oh shit baby! That shit feels fucking good! He groaned.

"Yes daddy, yes it does! I'm cumin!" Kandy-Cola screamed at the top of her lungs as he pushes her legs even farther back some more to her head and pounds away furiously.

"Ugghh, I'm cumin too!" He groaned as he releases a huge nut into her ass then collapsed on top of her.

"See I told you that you would like it. I'm ready for more." She said as she kisses his neck and felt his dick growing inside her and getting hard once.

Chapter 8

"I'm done Tatiana. I don't want to do any more dates." Juicy said while sitting in the passenger's seat of Tatiana's Mercedes Benz crying with tears running down her cheeks. Can we just stop now? My pussy is sore after letting those three men run a train on me." Juicy said.

"Juicy stop your fucking crying. I told you the dates with the black dudes are a little worse and that your pussy would get a little sore. You can do a quick stop in a hotel room and soak, it's nothing Epsom Salt and a douche can't fix, that pussy will be tight and feel brand new and ready for actions to get more money."Tatiana replied.

"I don't care Tatiana I'm tired and feel used up. I'm ready to go home, we made more than enough money." Juicy replied while crying.

"Listen, we have four more dates little sister, so you better shut up and get your act together and stop all that crying. I helped take care of you. It was me who finally called the cops so they can catch him in the act of raping us. It was me who testified when you were too scared to. It was me that made sure he got locked up for years to come so we can live a normal life and it was me that took care of you when mommy gave us to foster care to live in the system, because we got her man locked up, even though she should have went to jail as well. I don't ever want to hear you tell me no after all I've done and do for you Juicy. Tatiana said while staring at her sister.

Juicy wipes her tears away and looks at Tatiana.

Whatever! Let's just please get this night over with. She said with water in her eyes then pulls out her cell phone and began to text her best friend Marvin while Tatiana pulls off from the house they just came out of.

Yo, those bitches were some freaks. Especially the older one, the younger one looks like she wasn't into that shit. Jason said.

He was the owner of the house in Jamaica, Queens where Tatiana and Juicy had just left from. Tyrek, Jason, David and Russ were all best friends and on spring break from Long Island University.

"Man we need to do this again and it didn't even coast that much for us to run a train on them!"Russ said excitedly.

"Yea I'm down with that." Tyrek responded as they drink Grey Goose on ice.

The Stalker watches Tatiana's car pull off. When he was sure they were gone, he grabs the soft leather face mask off the passenger's side floor and puts it on zipping it up at the back then grabs the electric Taser and eighteen inch wooden paddle that was cover in black leather that had small metal spikes embedded on it.

He steps out his car and looks both ways. The sky was turning dark and had a pinkish color as the sun was going down. He didn't care that a few people stared at him from their car windows as they drove by. "They can't see my fucking face anyway." The Stalker thought to his self as he walks up the stairs to the front door of the house Juicy and Tatiana had left from.

"You never lie, word I want the same chicks to come by and freak off tomorrow night."David said, speaking for the first time.

FETISH

They didnt even notice that we recorded the whole thing. Jason said while setting up the mac book pro lap top to play the video he recorded.

He pressed a button that transferred the image to the 42 inch flat screen T.V. in the living room. They all sat on the couch. Moaning sounds boom from the loud T.V.

See, I told you that nigga David ate the older ones pussy and fucked her raw with no condom.

Ewww, youre a nasty ass nigga. Tyrek said causing the other two men to bust out laughing.

Nigga dont you know you should never fuck a prostitute without a condom. They take all kinds of dick from anyone, even your ugly fat ass. Thats their job. Jason said while laughing.

Yo I cant even front, my condom popped and I kept right on going inside the younger ones pussy. Tyrek replied.

Damn both of you niggas are nasty with dirty dicks. Russ said speaking for the first time and went back to watching T.V. He could see Juicy▯s facial expression balled up in pain while Tyrek and Jason took turns fucking her from the back doggy style.

The sound of the doorbell, made all the men jump.

▯Yo Russ, go get the door it▯s the pizza we ordered.▯Jason said in a demanding tone.

▯Schmmp! Why I have to answer the door? I want to finish watching the video of those chicks too.▯Russ responded.

▯Man just go answer the damn door, besides you have the shortest scenes out of all of us, your ass came in two minutes.▯Jason said while laughing.

Russ got off the couch and stomps off walking toward the front door. When he got there he looked through the small glass window that was in the middle of the wooden door.

▯Fellas you▯re not going to believe this, but there▯s some weird looking guy standing at the door with some kind of freaky leather mask on.▯Russ shouted over the loud moans coming from the T.V.

Nigga just open the door, it's probably Caden. I told him we were having some freaks over, but he made it here too late, that's his lost. I was only willing to pay for an hour and half of their time! Jason shouted.

I don't know if it's Caden. Russ said as he felt a bad vibe while still looking through the small window on the door at the man standing there.

He slowly opens the door.

Caden is that your weird ass? He asked as he inches the door open some more.

Ummm. The man in the doorway mumbles.

Russ steps back to open the door fully and as soon as he did he wished he hadn't. The Stalker raised his hand and placed the electric Taser onto Russ neck, sending 500 volts of electricity into his body.

Uggghhh! Russ made a gagging sound as his body went into convulsions and shook back and forth while he was standing up.

White foam came out his mouth, then his eye balls exploded oozing out red puss from his eyes sockets where his eyeballs use to be. Russ tries to scream, but couldn't as the electric volts stopped his heart. The Stalker caught Russ body as it was falling backwards and gently places him down on the floor being careful not to make a sound as he enters the house and shuts the front door.

Yo, I got the only damn bubbles in my gut. I'm going to take a shit. I'll be right back. Jason said while rubbing his stomach and getting up from the couch and walking out the living room.

He walks up a flight of stairs.

I bet it was him who was passing gas stinking up the place for the past hour. Tyrek said while laughing and causing David to laugh as well, while they continue to sit on the couch watching the video of Juicy and Tatiana.

The Stalker quietly steps deeper into the house with the leather paddle covered in metal spikes raised high. His eyes was opened wide with rage in them as he stops in his tracks and looks at the back of the two mens heads that was sitting in front of him. His eyes wander to the T.V. were he could see one of the men taking turns fucking Tatiana while she gave the next one head. Then Juicy on her back with her legs spread wide open as Tyrek pounds away while David leans close to her face, sticking his dick in and out of her mouth as if she was sucking on a blow pop. Juicy moans and jerks him off while sucking it at the same time. The Stalker had seen enough as tears water up in his eyes. Tyrek and David never heard the little bit of noise the Stalker made behind them.

The Stalker stares at Tyrek and knew he was the strongest of the two and most likely to be the one to put up the greatest fight. The Stalker raises the paddle even higher in the air, holding it with both hands and swung with all his might, whacking Tyrek on the back of his head with the paddle. Tyrek's neck buckle and he falls forward, face first onto the brown carpet. David turns his head to the side to see Tyrek on the floor.

Oh shit, are you okay? He asks then screams.

Ahhhh! Ahhhh! Ugghhaa! The Stalker whacks him in the mouth with the paddle, breaking and cracking a few of David's front teeth as he tries to scream and breathe at the same time.

He swallows his broken teeth, wraps his hand around his neck as he chokes on them. The Stalker whacks him on the forehead twice.

Ahhhh! Ahhhh! David tried to scream once more but was only able to get a funny sound out as the spikes from the paddle got stuck in his forehead.

The Stalker yanks free the paddle and swung it like a baseball bat. H

Home run! He shouted as the paddle connected with Davids pudgy face and sent his fat body off the couch, knocking him unconscious.

The Stalker grins through the black leather sex mask. He wasted no time to pull out some Japanese silk love rope, used for bondage. He hog ties Tyrek and David after stripping them naked.

Shut up! And keep it down, Im trying to concentrate.

Jason screams from the bathroom as he heard all the noise coming from downstairs along with moaning and grunting sounds coming from the living rooms T.V. The Stalker turns his head toward the sound of Jasons voice, while he was bent over tying up the last knot on the rope on David's feet. He picks up the paddle of the floor and walks to the staircase while looking at the pictures on the walls as he walks up the stairs.

Damn loud fuckers acting like they never made a home video of themselves before. Jason said as he sat on the toilet, reading a book on his Kindle Fire, called The Trap House, by Author Shameek Speight.

Ugghhh! My stomach is still bubbling, but I can't shit. What in the hell did I eat to make me so constipated? Jason said out loud to himself.

Aaaahhhh! He screams like a young girl in a high pitched tone and drops his Kindle when the bathroom door flew open from a powerful kick, and a man wearing a leather sex mask holding a paddle covered in black leather and tiny sharp metal spikes, dressed in all black, just standing in the doorway.

Jason couldn't see the man's mouth because the zipper over the mouth piece was zipped shut on the mask. But he could tell the man was smiling behind the mask from the look in his eyes. Jason had no idea who the stranger was, he cover his dick with his left hand and uses his right hand to pull up his jeans while continuing to scream like a little girl. The Stalker busts out laughing because Jason looked just like Kevin Hart down to his 5'2" even his facial expression and down to his voice. The Stalker swung twice, hitting Jason in the temple and ear.

"I have to make your ass stop screaming." The Stalker shouted while laughing insanely up under the mask and hits Jason four more times.

"Ahhhh! Ahhhh!" Jason hollered in fear and pain.

He puts up his left hand to block one of the blows to only have the paddle breaking four of his finger.

"Ahahahah! Stop please! Oh God make him stop!" Jason pleaded for his life while crying.

The Stalker swung the paddle like a psycho, hitting Jason over and over in the face and head. The Stalker stops suddenly.

"You and your friends didn't stop when you were messing with what belongs to me!" He Shouted.

FETISH

"I don't know what you're talking about!" Jason responded while lying with his face over the toilet bowl, coughing up thick blood mixed with saliva and blood leaking from his head like a faucet.

The two young ladies that were here not too long ago, that you and your friends treated like sluts and recorded what you've done to them! The Stalker shouted through clenched teeth.

He unzips the zipper by the mouth area so he could speak more clearly.

"How were we supposed to know? I call the older one all the time when I come home from school it's what she does for a living. Man, please don't kill me for the choice she made." Jason pleaded.

"Hmmm, you have a point. I'll give you one chance to save your life. Get up!" The Stalker said while using the paddle to lift up Jason's chin out of the toilet.

"Ugghhh!" Jason grunts in pain.

His rib cage was cracked, four of his fingers were broken and blood kept leaking into his eyes from his forehead. Jason grunted in

FETISH

agony pain as the Stalker pushes him down the stairs to the first floor. Jason's eyes opens up wide as he fought the feeling of wanting to scream all over again as he stares at what used to be Russ head smashed in and cracked open. His brain was oozing out of black holes where his eyes used to be. Jason then looks at David and Tyrek butt naked hogtied with their hands and feet tied in the air behind them. Tyrek was still unconscious, but David was squirming around, trying to break free until he looks up and sees them.

I got bored and think I over did it with the guy who answered the front door. I think Russ was his name. The Stalker said with a sick twisted smile on his face.

Jason's heart raced even faster, pounding hard, staring at the leather sex mask on the Stalker face, sent a petrifying feeling through Jason and David's bodies.

Listen I'm going to give you that one chance to save your piece of shit life, like I promised you. All you have to do is kill your two friends here and you're free to go. You can even tell the police I forced you to do it. The Stalker said with a sinister grin on his face.

"You want me to what? I can't do that man, they're my best friends." Jason said with tears mixed with blood running down his cheek.

"Okay then you will die with them!" The Stalker shouted as he raises the paddle high ready to strike Jason over the head.

"No! Wait! Wait! Please don't hit me! I'll do it." Jason cried out while using his forearms to cover his face the best he could.

"What did you say?" The Stalker said and stops in the middle of swing.

"I said I'll do it, just don't hit me again." Jason said in a terrified tone as his body trembles nervously in fear.

"So it's a deal then." The Stalker replied while smiling.

"Yes it's a deal." Jason said as he moves his forearms from his face.

"Good! Here take this!" The Stalker said passing Jason the paddle.

Jason's looks at the paddle that was covered in metal spikes soaked with his and his friend's blood in disbelief, as if the Stalker was trying to trick him.

⬛Here, take it!⬜ The Stalker demanded pushing the paddle into Jason's right hand.

⬛Now I want you to stick the handle of the paddle in this one's ass then beat him with the paddle over his head, until you see his brain.⬜ The Stalker said pointing too Tyrek who was still unconscious.

David looked up at Jason and shook his head no but dared not to speak.

⬛You want me to do what?⬜ Jason said with his facial expression twisted up in pain and sorrow.

⬛You fucking heard me!⬜ The Stalker shouted.

Jason walked weakly over behind the couch next to the flat screen T.V. on the wall, where Tyrek was butt naked hog tied on the floor. Jason looked at the Stalker as he bends down, and looked as if he wanted to start crying all over again.

⬛Do it!⬜ The Stalker shouted and his eyes looked as if they were going to pop out through the leather face mask he had on.

The sound of his voice scared Jason so much he reacted without thinking or knowing it. Pushing the handle of the paddle with all the might he had left into Tyrek's ass.

"Aaaahhh! What the fuck!" Tyrek screamed as he regained consciousness, confused from the new found pain traveling through his body.

He wiggled and squirmed, trying to break free of the tight ropes but couldn't. He clenched his butt cheeks and tried to push the handle of the paddle out of his anus but felt it go deeper inside.

"Aaaahhhh! Aaaahhhh!" He hollered in excruciating pain as his anus began to rip opened.

His blood splashed into Jason's face rapidly.

"Ewww! Ugghhh! Shit!" Jason complained as he wiped the blood off his face, the smell of feces was in the air.

"Finish the job now!" The Stalker delegated in a deep voice.

Jason walks back over to Tyrek with pain balled up on his face as tears flow down his cheeks. Tyrek's body felt pain like he never felt before. He fought back his tears, as he was violated wanting to kill the person, who just stuck the handle of the paddle in his rectum, ripping it.

"Jason, why are you doing this? I swear I am going to kill your ass as soon as I get free." Not fully understanding the situation he was in and how serious it was.

"I am sorry Tyrek I have to do this." Jason said while crying.

"Wait! Wait! We are best friends, don't do it man, please untie me!" Tyrek pleased seeking mercy from a man he once called a friend.

"You're taking too long, I have things to do. Smash his fucking head open, in return for your life!" The Stalker shouted staring at Jason with a do, or get done degrading look.

Jason looked at the Stalker's beaded eyes, with his leather sex mask on, and his body began to shake.

"Don't do it Jason man, don't listen to him. We are friends and I've known you my entire life. We grew up together. Don't do it, you are stronger than this!☐ Tyrek shouted while crying and trying to wiggle free from the silk rope he was hogtied in.

☐Do it! Fucking Do it!☐The Stalker yelled. ☐You motherfucking pussy, just smash his head.☐

Jason in a frightened state repeated. ☐I☐m sorry, I☐m sorry!☐To Tyrek as he closed his eyes tightly, and raised the paddled high above his head with his right hand and came down with all his might.

☐Ugghhh! Ahhhh! Ahhhh! Jason why? Why? I am your best friend!☐

Jason listened to Tyrek☐s cries with every blow he made to his head. A lot of popping and cracking sounds echoed throughout the living room, as Tyrek screams and cries for Jason to stop, to finally come to an end. As Jason opened his eyes slowly and looked up at the Stalker, he noticed the Stalker was grinning, while licking his lips between the sick insane look on his face and the sex leather mask. Jason wanted to start crying all over again. He stood bent over with the paddle in his hand, scared to look down. He slowly and insecurely looked down at his friend Tyrek who had stopped twitching and screaming.

Ahhhh! Ahhhh! Ahhhh! Lord no! Jason hollered as he looked down and saw the most horrifying thing he ever saw.

The paddle was turned sideways splitting the back of Tyrek's head, revealing his brain matters and pieces of crushed skull was splattered everywhere, along with a big pool of blood. Tears pour out of Jason's eyes, as he made a funny face gasping, covering his nose. He bent over vomiting on the brown living room carpet.

Good! Good! Now the next one and you will have your miserable life. The Stalker stated.

No, I can't, I just can't Jason said with spit mixed with vomit dripping from his mouth, while still bent over. The smell of his vomit mixed with the smell of Tyrek's feces made the Stalker's stomach bubble with disgust.

I told you I don't have time to waste, either you kill your other friend or you die with him as well! The Stalker shouted, as he looks at the G-Shock watch on his wrist.

He knew that he was running out of time and had to catch up to Tatiana and Juicy.

⬚Why? Why are you doing this to us?⬚ Jason said in a whining tone and a mouth full of spit.

The Stalker walks over to him and then right hooks him then hits him with a left punch, sending Jason crashing into the floor.

⬚Finish the fucking job and kill your fat friend or you will be next. Y⬚all done fucked up and touched something that only belongs to me!⬚

⬚Please don⬚t hit me anymore. I⬚l do it.⬚ Jason groaned as he eases off the floor.

His left hand was badly swollen, and four of his fingers were broken, every time he moved it he felt like crying. He used his right hand to grab the handle of the paddle and tried to lift it up, but couldn⬚t.

⬚It⬚s stuck.⬚He whined, while looking at the Stalker trying not to look down at his dead best friend.

⬚Stop being such a girl, step on what⬚s left of your friends head and pull the fucking paddle out of it!⬚ The Stalker said in a demanding tone.

Jason's facial expression was balled up in distress. He steps on Tyrek's head and pulls the paddle with all his might and made a grunting sound as he lifts it up and heard a cracking sound.

I got it. He said excited, then looks at the black leather paddle stuck on the side of it on to the spikes was half of Tyrek's face.

His eye balls seemed to be moving, looking at Jason and scanning the room from side to side.

Holy, shit! Oh shit! Ahhhh! Ahhhh! Jason screams as he shook the paddle and the half of Tyrek's face flew off.

Ha! Ha! Ha! The Stalker laughs.

Now kill your other friend so I can get the hell out of here. The Stalker said as he points his left finger down in the direction of where David was tied up at, but when he and Jason looked David wasn't there at all.

What the fuck! Where did he go? The Stalker shouted.

David had seen more than enough as he watched Jason crack open the head of one of their best friends. He quickly stopped crying and waited until the Stalker and Jason were distracted and tries to break out of the silk red ropes he was tied up in. When that failed, he remembered an old school dance called the Worm it's when the dancer lay flat on the floor and moves his body around bouncing like a worm. David danced and moved his body just like the worm, moving his stomach in and out, while wiggling and his body does a slight hop.

'Yes!' He mumbled in a low tone as his heart races and he inches his way all the way into the kitchen.

'God just let me get to a knife or something to free myself.' David said out loud to himself as he leans to the side and bumps the kitchen cabinet repeatedly. A butter knife that was by the sink falls onto his back. 'Ouch!' He groaned and moves his fingers around trying to reach the butter knife.

The Stalker heard the noise from David bumping into the cabinets.

'He's in the kitchen! Get him!' The Stalker shouted while following Jason towards the kitchen.

'What am I doing? I got this paddle in my possession. He has no weapons and I can *take him, even if he's taller and bigger than me. I fought bigger dudes and won.'* Jason told himself as he builds up his courage.

He took a step and spins around, stretching out his right arm that held the paddle. The Stalker didn't see what Jason was up to until it was too late. He tries to lean back and dodge the paddle but it slams into his neck.

Ugghhh! He made a gagging sound as he chokes on air and his own saliva. He grabs his neck as he tries to breathe.

Jason swung once more, hitting The Stalker on the side of his face, sending him flying straight to the ground.

You bastard, this is for Tyrek! Jason shouted as he hits the Stalker in the center of his back hitting him in his spinal cord.

Ahahah! Ugghhhh! The Stalker screamed as his body bounces a little hitting the floor and he just stops moving lying flat.

Jason took off running toward the kitchen. He stops when he saw David's fat body hogtied squirming around.

FETISH

"Please no, don't kill me." David cried out when he heard footsteps approaching his way.

"Shhhh, it's me David, I got him." Jason said as he drops the paddle and picks up the butter knife off of David's back.

He saws away at the silk ropes until they pop, setting David free.

"You got him? Who the hell was that maniac? Did you kill him?" David asks as he rubs his sore wrist that hurt from the ropes being so tight on them.

"Yea, I think he's dead. I hit him until he stopped moving." Jason responded.

"What? You didn't beat him until you saw blood, or until you knew for sure you killed him?" David responded with a panic look on his face.

"No but he was unconscious. I knocked his ass out cold." Jason replied.

"What? You just knocked him out? You're ass never seen a damn horror movie, you don't stop shooting or beating the killer until you see blood fool. Or they will come back." David said while sweating profusely.

FETISH

Man shut up, this is not a movie, let's just find our cell phones and call the police and can your fat ass put some clothes on, because it feels funny talking to you naked and watching your fat gut stomach jiggle. Jason said in disgust while shaking his head.

They both stood up. Jason picks up the leather paddle and grips it tight with his right hand. They walk through the kitchen door and walks into the living room, they stop by the loveseat with their facial expression twisted up in horror, mixed with sadness and pain as they stare at their dead friend Tyrek hogtied with his head split open in half with his face missing. His brains and blood was oozing out onto the carpet. Jason looks at the other half of Tyrek's face that was by the T.V. that had gotten stuck on the spikes on the leather paddle.

Oh God! He groaned as he held his stomach as he continues to stare at the piece of his friend's eyes and lips seem to be still moving.

Ugghhh! Jason grunted as vomit travels up from his stomach to his throat and flew out onto the floor.

⬛I had no choice he made me, he made me do it!⬛Jason repeated over and over while holding his stomach bent over throwing up.

⬛I know man I saw the whole thing and I⬛l tell the police that when they come but now we need to get the hell out of here.⬛David said while looking for his clothes but only found Tyrek⬛s clothes that were too small and tight fitting for him. He digs around in Tyrek⬛s jean pockets and found his iPhones 4S.

⬛Here⬛s a phone. Call the cops!⬛David said as he works his way into Tyrek⬛s boxer⬛s that hugged his skin.

Jason puts down the paddle onto the love seat and looks at David with the tight boxers with a blank stare.

⬛Really that⬛s a damn shame, those shits look like pum pum shorts.⬛Jason said while taking the phone out of David⬛s hand and dials 911.

⬛What? I can⬛t find my clothes. I had to put on something.⬛David replied and shrugs his shoulders.

"Ummm, where did you say you left the crazy guy knocked out at?"David asked as he looks around.

Jason's mouth opens wide in horror as his body began to tremble. He was laying right there!"Jason said pointing to a spot behind the long couch and was mad at his self as he just now realizes the Stalker was gone.

"Hello 911 what is your emergency?" Jason heard the operator say on the other line.

"See I told you man, I fucking told you this always happen in the movies. You're supposed to make sure he was dead!"David shouted then froze up with his mouth opened.

"Don't worry about it, I'm on the phone with the police now and what in the hell is wrong with you? Why you look like that?" Jason said as he stares at the dumb facial expression David had while pointing his finger.

"Ahahahahah!" David screamed as he watched the Stalker sneak up behind Jason and grabs the paddle off the loveseat without making a sound.

"Why in the hell are you screaming?" Jason asks and turns around to look behind himself.

Before he could realize what was going on the Stalker swung the paddle with all his might sending it crashing into the side of Jason's face breaking the hand he was using to hold the phone to his ear and sent him flying sideways at the same time.

"You fucking Kevin Heart look-alike!" The Stalker shouted as he leaps up into the air and came down swinging onto Jason's chest.

The sound of his ribcage breaking echoes through the living room. One of his broken ribcage bones pierces his lung, jamming deep inside it. Jason's eyes opened wide as he chokes on his own blood that seeks out the corners of his eyes and mouth. He tries to scream be couldn't. It sounded more like a gagging noise.

"All you had to do was complete your end of the fucking deal and I would've spared your life!"Was the last thing he heard as the paddle came crashing down onto his face, smashing it in breaking every bone in his face.

His body went in to convulsions as it shook and jerked, and he finally dies.

⌐Ahahahah!⌐ David hollered and had seen more than enough.

He took off running towards the back door. He fumbles with the door knob out of nervousness, then finally got the door open and zoomed out the back door while still screaming. His fat stomach and men breast bounced up and down. The Stalker looks up from what used to be Jason⌐s face and took off running, following David⌐s loud screams. David ran through a few bushes then opens a gate and was now in the front yard, he slowed down to catch his breath. Being overweight and just running longer than ten footsteps made him tried.

'Huh!' He said out loud to himself as he heard a noise coming from the bushes in the backyard.

⌐Oh shit!⌐David shouted as his eyes felt like they were going to pop out his socket as he looks back and could see the Stalker running towards him at full speed with the paddle that was dripping in blood in his hand and smiling with the sex leather mask on his face.

FETISH

⌐Ahhhh! Ahhhh!⌐ David hollered and took off running down the sidewalk.

⌐Help! Help me!⌐ He screamed as he looks around, looking behind him while still running and could see the Stalker right on his tail.

⌐Help me please! Help me!⌐ Ouch! Ouch!⌐He screamed as the Stalker chases him and whacks him on his butt cheeks with the paddle.

A few cars that was driving by slows down, curious of what was going on as they watch a fat man with braids in his hair, running bare foot down the street with white boxers on that looked like pum pum shorts, and a man dressed in an all-black leather body suit with a full leather sex mask on, smacking the man on the ass. People slowed down in their cars and pulls out their cell phones and records what is going on.

⌐Oh this is so going on YouTube.⌐A guy said as he sat in the back seat of his friends ride.

⌐Why wonⅠt you help me? Help me please!⌐David screams as he panics and ran up to one of the cars and bangs on the window.

⬛This shit is crazy, just like something you would see in one of those jackass movies.⬜ The driver of the car said as he pulls off leaving David standing there out of breath.

⬛Why won⬛t anyone help me? Please help me! Help me!⬜David shouted at the top of his lungs as he ran to another car full of people and bangs on the window.

The teenagers inside the car bust out laughing while watching his fat body jiggle like Jell-O and they record him with their smartphones.

⬛Do you think he⬛s serious and really needs help?⬜ The young woman said in the passenger⬛s seat while still recording David banging on the window.

⬛Naw, this is some kind of a joke for Halloween.⬜ The driver said.

The Stalker ran up on David and swung the paddle with all his might, whacking him in the center of his back.

⬛Aaaaahhhh!⬜ David hollered in excruciating pain as the stinging feeling travels through his body and the metal spikes on the paddle rips away bits and pieces of his flesh when the Stalker pulls it away.

⟦Oh shit!⟧The teenagers in the car all said simultaneously as their eyes opened wide with shock and horror.

David collapsed to his knees.

⟦You thought your chunky ass could get away from me. You were better off begging for your life fat boy!⟧The Stalker said as he stares down at David.

⟦No please don⟧t kill me man, I⟧m sorry. I want to live and go home to my mommy.⟧ David pleads with his facial expression balled up in pain as tears stream down his chubby cheeks.

⟦I want to live!⟧He screams as he cried hysterically.

⟦Whack!⟧Was the only sound you can hear echoing through the streets mix with David⟧s cries as the Stalker swung the paddle repeatedly. He swung hard and hit David in the mouth. The metal spikes got stuck into his face.

FETISH

"Ahhhh! Ahhhh!" The teenagers and other people in their cars screamed in horror as they continue to watch and record everything with their phones as they realize what they were now watching wasn't a prank it was real.

The Stalker tries to yank the paddle away but couldn't. The spikes had penetrated deep into David's face. He pulls even harder and the paddle broke free of David's face taking his top lip with it.

"Ahhhh! Ahhhh!" The people in their cars hollered as they look at the mouth dangling from the paddle.

"Ahhhh! Ugghhh!" David's scream came out in a funny gagging sound as blood pour out where his top lip should have been.

He held his mouth.

"Help me! Help me please!" He mumbles.

The car filled with the teenagers that was closest to him the diver rolled down the window and stuck his head out of it.

"Hey leave him alone, we're recording everything and we are going to call the..."

before he could finish his sentence the paddle whacks him across the face three times.

◻Agghhh! Agghhh!◻ He hollered as his head twisted from side to side with each blow.

Then he stops moving with his head hanging out the driver◻s side window.

◻Ahhhh! Ahhhh!◻ The woman in the passenger◻s seat screams as she looks at her friend barely breathing and his eyeball◻s hanging out of the eye sockets, only connected to his socket by a thin piece of flesh as it bounces up and down.

David turns around on his heels and knees and quickly starts clawing away while the Stalker was distracted.

◻Where do you think you◻re going, fat ass?◻ The Stalker said as he whacks him on the ass.

◻Ahhhh! Ahhhh!◻ David screams as the Stalker flips the paddle sideways and swung it with all his strength at the back of David◻s neck.

A loud crushing sound echoes through the street, unable to move his arms and legs.

"Lord forgive me, and welcome me in your arms and warm embrace." David mumbles as the paddle came crashing down on his head, repeatedly until it cracks open and brain matter and large pieces lay on the street.

"Ahhhh! Ahhhh! Ahhhh!" The people in the cars that witnessed the whole thing and recorded it, pulls off while calling the police.

The teenagers hops out the car and took off running leaving their friend hanging out the driver's side window. The Stalker smiles as he looks at David's body twitching and head slashed like a bug that's been stepped on. The Stalker took off running and runs back into the house down the block. He took one last look at the dead three men in the living room then grabs the laptop with the video of Juicy and Tatiana on it. He ran out the house as he heard police sirens closing in from a block away. He hops in his car and quickly removes the leather sex mask and starts up his car. His heart pounds with fear as police cars pulled up in front of the house he was just in.

"We're looking for a suspect wearing all-black and a freaky looking leather sex mask!"

FETISH

The Stalker heard a police officer shout as he slowly pulls off and made a left turn as more police cars zoom towards him.

Chapter 9

Kandy-Cola took another bird bath for the night and used her hands to straighten out her red Louis Vuitton dress before stepping out the master bathroom in Casino-Rich's bedroom.

'This is too easy, I already got him turned out doing all type of shit to his ass. It's just a matter of time before he's stuck on me that he won't know left from right. I'll have him that fucked up in the head. Hmmm $50,000 a month isn't bad at all and more than I'm used to, but he's worth more, he's a damn millionaire. So, for having myself on his arms is going to cost him a lot more.' Kandy-Cola thought to herself as she watches Casino-Rich get dressed and tie up his laces.

His Goonz Squad chain swung from side to side. He looks up at Kandy-Cola standing by the bathroom doorway and had to grin as he stares with lust at her perfect thick voluptuous body.

'Damn, sex with her is even better than I could image.' He thought to himself.

I see you're looking flawless once again. So I take it that you're ready to go, so we can tear this city up and let the world know Ms. Kandy-Cola now belongs to me. Casino-Rich said.

Kandy-Cola walks seductively towards him and place her lips onto his and kisses him deeply, their tongues dance in each other's mouths.

Damn, you really need to stop or we'll never be able to leave this house. He groaned as he felt his manhood grow in his jeans, trying to break free.

Kandy-Cola grabs his hard dick through his jeans.

That wouldn't be such a bad thing. She said seductively, while licking her lips and releasing her grip and walks to the door.

Casino-Rich looks at her thick juicy butt cheeks switch from side to side.

No it wouldn't be a bad idea. He mumbled as he follows her out the bedroom.

Club Perfections was jumping, everybody who was anybody was there. Perfections wasn't your typical club, the design of the club had stripper poles everywhere in the club with the best looking strippers in New York City dancing there, mixed with club people. Rappers from around the world came to relax and pop bottles of Champagne. The line to get inside of the hottest club in Queens, New York wrapped around the block with people dressed at their best.

A lime green Lamborghini pulls in front of the club followed by twelve 745 B.M.W.s and one red Aston Martin. The lime green Lamborghini doors cut up through the air like a knife, swinging up. The crowd of people on the long line turned their heads and broke their necks to see what crew was making such an extravagant entrance. All they could see was a pair of Red Bottom, Louboutin shoes step out the driver side with a beautiful thick brown skin complexion leg attached to it. Then Kandy-Cola steps out the Lamborghini and Casino-Rich steps out the passengers side. DWes, Casino-Richs main personal bodyguard steps out of a 745 B.M.W. and quickly made his way in front of Casino-Rich and Kandy-Cola, using his massive body size to protect them as people in the line recognized it was the famous Casino-Rich and the Goonz Squad. Women began to holler and scream out of excitement.

FETISH

⬛Oh my God, it⬛s Casino-Rich!⬛One of the women shouted so loud it felt like it would bust a few of the other people in line eardrums. Then she pass out, her date catches her in his arms just before she hit the ground.

⬛Hey Kandy how are you?⬛One of the huge bouncers at the door said as she approaches the front door of the club.

⬛Hey Bear, how are you?⬛Kandy-Cola replied.

⬛I⬛m fine sweetie, it⬛s been a while. I see you⬛re rolling deep tonight.⬛Bear responded.

⬛Yea they⬛re my people, the Goonz Squad.⬛Kandy-Cola replied.

Bear looks down at the platinum choke collar chain on her neck with the green encrusted diamond Goonz Squad medallion then looks at Casino-Rich who was covered in diamonds with his giant entourage behind him. By being a professional bouncer for a living, Bear was far from impressed. He see⬛s rappers and celebrities everyday come to the club. The club was full of them now.

⬛Yo, I see you and my woman are real cool and all that but we⬛re trying to get up in here fast with no issues and there's a little extra something, something in it for you and the other bouncers if there's no pat down. If you know what I mean. Casino-Rich said cutting into the conversation.

No homie, I don't know what you mean, and don't care who you are! Your whole team will have to be searched! Bear shouted crossing his arms and showing his muscles.

D'Wes steps up in Bear's face and Casino-Rich pulls out his gun from his waist and his entourage pulls out.

Nigga watch your fucking mouth my people and I will light this mother fucking place up and nobody will be able to party. Casino-Rich said with venom.

Wow! Hahahaha! That's tough talk Mr., but playboy it may work in whatever city or state you're from but you're in Queens, New York my nigga. The bouncer said while laughing then grins.

Then two more bouncers came out with an entourage of thugs behind them, armed with shotguns and handguns. Then more came out from buildings across the street. The Goonz Squad quickly found themselves surrounded and out gunned, but they showed no signs of fear or backing down.

⬚Bear and Casino calm down gentlemen. There⬚s no need to see who has the biggest dick or guns. We all just came out to have a good time. This is the deal Bear, the Goonz Squad is going to give up their guns or put them in their cars, all but Casino-Rich and his right hand and bodyguard D⬚Wes. You have to respect that.⬚Kandy-Cola said while licking her lips seductively then digs in her purse and pulls out a stack of hundred dollar bills.

She knew it was a thousand dollars. She stuffs it into Bear⬚s pocket. Bear grills Casino-Rich and his people a little longer.

⬚Okay Kandy, just because we go way back. Don⬚t make me regret this Cola.⬚ Bear stated.

⬚Baby you do all of that!⬚ Casino-Rich shouted as his pride ate away at him.

⬚Calm down baby it⬚s a small thing to a giant, big daddy.⬚Kandy-Cola said stroking his wounded pride as she kisses him deeply.

When they broke their embrace Casino-Rich puts his gun back on his waist then raises his hand making a sign, telling his Goonz Squad to put their guns back in their vehicles. Casino-Rich continues to stare down Bear as he steps into the club with DWes and Alonzo by his side with Kandy-Cola leading the way and soon after the Goonz Squad enters.

People in the club scream as they recognize Casino-Rich and showed love to Kandy-Cola. She was well known in the Club Circuit and throughout New York City. A host leads them to their own V.I.P. section. The DJ from Hot 97.1 was in the DJ booth. People were on the dance floor, shaking their asses as if there was no tomorrow, to a Nicki Minaj song, 'Beez in the Trap'.

Strippers of all shapes and sizes were sliding up and down on the poles that were spread out throughout the club.

Casino-Rich and Alonzo got in the mood right away feeling the vibe. They ordered bottles of Champagne and Vodka, the Goonz Squad members grab a few women that were standing outside the V.I.P. area dying to get in.

The host V.J. Larry came into the V.I.P. area and smiles when he sees Kandy-Cola. He made his way through the crowd of people dancing in the V.I.P. area.

FETISH

⌈Oh shit, if it isnⱦ the famous hard to tame Kandy-Cola, chilling with the Goonz Squad and the hottest rapper out this year, Casino-Rich.⌉ V.J. Larry said into the small microphone in his hand that was live, hooked up to Hot 97.1ꜱ radio station.

Casino-Rich puts his arm around Kandy-Cola as they sat on the black couch with a table full of bottles of liquor in front of them.

⌈Sheꜱ not only chilling with the Goonz Squad, Kandy-Cola is now my wifey and first female member of the Goonz Squad and is now off the market to all those fake ass thug rappers! Sheꜱ rolling with real Gꜱ!⌉ Casino-Rich shouted in to the microphone.

V.J. Larryꜱ eyes open up wide as he grows hyped.

⌈Really, this canⱦ be. Has somebody finally locked down the sexy Ms. Kandy-Cola?⌉ V.J. Larry said and places the microphone next to her mouth.

⌈Yes itꜱ true. Casino-Rich is now my hubby and proud to say it and I hope soon heⱦl be so much more.⌉ She said while smiling, revealing a set of pearly white teeth.

□Oh my God I need a picture with you two.□V.J. Larry said showing how hyped and excited he was to be the first to broadcast the news to the Hip Hop world.

When a photographer walks through the V.I.P. area, V.J. Larry flags him down. Kandy-Cola and Casino-Rich stood up and posed for a few pictures that came out perfect.

□You heard it first people. Casino-Rich and Kandy-Cola are now an official couple and off the market.□ V.J. Larry said into the microphone and walks off to mingle with more celebrities.

The word of Kandy-Cola and Casino-Rich being a couple travels faster than lightening, club goers took pictures of them and posts it on YouTube and Facebook, even Twitter.

□I have to go to the bathroom baby.□ Kandy-Cola whispered into Casino-Rich□s ear.

It seemed like just a touch of her lips next to his body turned him on, but he knew he had to play it cool.

□Alright, Alonzo is going to follow you just to protect you if any of these clowns in here act up.⬛Casino-Rich replied over the loud music while dancing.

Kandy-Cola laughs.

⬛Please, this is my town baby, I keep telling you, people know what time it is, she said as she opens her purse and shows him the chrome 3.80 that rested next to her Mac makeup kit and a stacks of money.

⬛I feel you, but still you⬛re my woman now, that means my responsibility. So you have to have one of my peoples watching your back at all times, and I never thanked you for how you handled that situation outside. You didn⬛t have to hit that bouncer off. That⬛s my job and if he would⬛ve kept pushing the issue and acting tough, this place would⬛ve got shot down. I⬛ll repay you the money you gave him.⬛ Casino-Rich said.

⬛It⬛s nothing baby you can pay me back in other ways.⬛Kandy-Cola said as she kisses him on the lips and got up from the couch.

'I don't know why men got to be so damn hard headed. He knew damn well him and his team was outnumbered and gunned. It was a losing fight. I guess it's a male pride thing, but too much pride can get you killed.'

Kandy-Cola thought to herself as she works her way through the crowd of dancing people and it seemed as if every man in the club was trying to get her attention, grabbing her hand or arm.

No thank you. I'm good. She said loud over the music as guys try to holler at her.

She looks back and noticed Casino-Rich's right hand man Alonzo following her and grilling dudes, staring them down that was trying to talk to her.

'Damn, I told this nigga I can roll by myself I don't need one of his Goonz all up in my ass following me like a lost puppy.' She said to herself over the loud music as men continue to try to get her attention and she made her way into the bathroom.

A few of the women in the bathroom looks at her with hate and envy in their eyes and whisper amongst each other. Kandy-Cola went into a bathroom stall and shuts the door and pulls out her cellphone from her purse and dials a number.

Hey bitch, what are you up to? Tatiana said.

I'm getting it how I live boo. You know our motto money over niggas. You won't believe how much paper I got out of Casino-Rich. Kandy-Cola replied.

Word, tell me! Tatiana said excitedly.

I'll tell you when I get home later. I'm out at Club Perfections now. Kandy-Cola replied.

Your ass didn't tell me you were going clubbing tonight! I could have been making some money off his crew instead of messing with my usual tricks. I need new clientele. I got Juicy with me and she's whining on almost every date we go on tonight. Tatiana responded while shaking her head.

Girl you know making sure my position was secure before I bring any of you freaks around, but I'm good now so the next get together I'll make sure you're there. Kandy-Cola said.

You better bitch, I'll get up with you later sweetie I got more money to chase. Love you and be safe heifer. Tatiana said.

I love you too bitch and you be safe as well. Kandy-Cola replied then hangs up.

She looks up from her phone in shock to see the bathroom stall fly open and Alonzo standing there with his brown Texas fitted hat pulled low.

Nigga what the fuck are you doing? This is the woman's bathroom! Kandy-Cola shouted with an attitude.

You been in here for a while, I got worried. Alonzo replied as he steps into the stall and shuts the door.

So you come into the ladies bathroom! Nigga open the stall door and let me out, I don't need any of these hater groupie bitches getting any ideas and spreading rumors! Kandy-Cola said with her facial expression balled up in anger as she tries to squeeze pass him in the tight stall.

Wait, hold up. What's the rush baby girl? Alonzo said grabbing her by the arm.

You're the only bad woman in this club, not even one of them comes close to your body. Your body looks as if God himself made it. Alonzo stated.

FETISH

⌐So what, nigga tell me something I don⌐t know. Now move out my way.⌐ Kandy-Cola responded.

⌐Well what you don⌐t know is that I want you. Nobody has to know it can be our little secret. You won⌐t be the first of Casino-Rich⌐s women I hooked up with on the low.⌐Alonzo said with a huge grin on his face and zips down his zipper and pulls out his dick.

Kandy-Cola looks into his eyes then down at his manhood.

⌐Hahahhaha!⌐ She busts out laughing. Hahahaha! Is this a joke, is Ashton Kutcher going to jump out with camera and say I got ⌐Punk⌐d⌐ because you can⌐t be serious right? Hehehe!⌐ Kandy-Cola said while giggling and covering her mouth.

Rage travels through Alonzo⌐s body and could almost see the fire in him.

⌐Bitch, what⌐s so damn funny? This isn⌐t a fucking joke. You think you⌐re too good for me huh? He shouted and wraps his hand around her neck and began to squeeze.

⌐You⌐re going to give me that pussy one way or another, even if I have to take it!⌐He shouted while squeezing tighter on her neck and holding his dick with his other hand jerking it back and forth.

Kandy-Cola held her composure as she calmly stuck her hand in to her purse and grabs the chrome 3.80 handgun. Then stuck the barrel of the gun onto the head of Alonzo's dick and cocked the hammer with her thumb. Alonzo heard the sound of the gun cocking and looks down. His heart began to race.

Nigga get your fucking dirty hands off me. Kandy-Cola said through clenched teeth.

Alonzo's eyes were wide opened. He releases his grip and puts his hands up in the air.

Nigga I don't know what kind of woman you're used to but I'm not it. If you ever raise or put your hands on me again I will kill your fucking ass without hesitation. Kandy-Cola said looking him dead in the eyes so he would know she was serious.

You're just like every other lame dude. You get all mad because a bitch doesn't want you. Let me break it down to you little nigga. So your small mind doesn't get it confused. I am somebody and you're a no body. I only fuck bosses and let them taste this pussy. You are a worker with no dreams or goals and will forever be a worker. You're a little nigga eating off some real man's plate. Everything you have is because of Casino-Rich and yet you're trying to fuck his woman behind his back, you disloyal bastard. I'm not going to tell him how stupid you really are this time, but if you pull that shit again, we will see the outcome. Now get the fuck out my way pussy! Kandy-Cola said and brush past him out of the stall.

Oh yea, I wear heels longer than your dick. She said with a huge smile on her face as she looks down at his dick hanging out through the zipper pocket.

All the women in the bathroom heard her comment and busts out laughing.

Alonzo felt as if his soul and pride all in one had had be crushed. No one had ever pulled his cards like that before in his life. What really made it hurt was that everything she had said was true. He was just a worker even if he was Casino-Rich's right hand man and he wouldn't have shit if it weren't for him.

'That stuck up bitch, I'll get her ass, but I need to do some digging around and really find out something I can use on her stuck up ass.'

FETISH

Alonzo thought to himself as he pulls out his iPhone and began texting while walking out the woman's bathroom, with the agonizing laughter from the woman in there.

Kandy-Cola works her way back to the V.I.P. area and felt as if all eyes were on her and they were. Rappers and movie stars along with other men couldn't help but be mesmerized by her voluptuous body.

Casino-Rich kisses her deeply and passionately.

"Mmmm." She moaned as she became wet, but knew the real motive behind his kiss.

'Men are all the same they always want to mark their territory.' She thought to herself and smiled.

"It's almost time for us to break out of here baby." Casino-Rich said in her ear because the music was so loud.

"Why? We just got here daddy. You're not still upset about the thing with the bouncer out front are you?" She replied into his ear, while taking a sip of Moet Rose.

"Nah, not at all baby, but we should leave right now." Casino-Rich said.

Kandy-Cola looks at him and could see a huge evil grin on his face that she never saw before now. Then rapid gun fire went off in and outside the club. Kandy-Cola and Casino-Rich got low as people began to scream and holler and run for the exits.

⌐Let⌐s go!⌐ Casino-Rich shouted as he grabs her by the arm and his bodyguard D⌐Wes ran through the crowd like a football player, knocking people out of the way, leading and making a path for Casino-Rich and Kandy-Cola.

Kandy-Cola trips on something and looks down to see two dead women who had bullet holes in their foreheads, then she sees three dead men covered in blood and after a man shot but squirming around while people was stepping on him trying to save their own lives and get out the club.

Kandy-Cola thought she could never been so happier to smell fresh air and be outside, as she exits the club. People ran down the block and across the street hopping into their vehicles, while screaming and staying low. Something caught the corner of her eyes on the sidewalk.

"Ahhhh! Ahhhh! Ahhhh!"She screamed as she watched the bouncer Bear coughing up blood as he lay on the floor with his chest filled with over twenty bullet holes.

Kandy-Cola ran over to him.

"Bear you're going to be okay." She said.

"No he won't" Casino-Rich said as he ran over and kicks Bear in the jaw.

"Come the fuck on, we have to go!" Casino-Rich shouted as he grabs her once more and pulls her across the street and then they hop in the green Lamborghini.

She ducks low in the passenger seat as the sound of more gun fire roars throughout the street. She peep her head up as the Lamborghini speeds down the block and could see a man standing over Bear and empties a gun into his face.

"We're safe now." Casino-Rich said as they drove out of Queens, heading for Long Island.

Kandy-Cola sat quiet, lost in her thoughts and still stuck in shock at what just happened. She took a deep breath before speaking.

⌐Ummm! Were you behind all that shooting that went on?⌐ She asked while staring at him.

Casino-Rich turns his head and smiled like the cat that swallowed the canary and continues to drive.

Chapter 10

Juicy's heart ached. All she wanted to do was go home. I made more than enough money, but Tatiana doesn't want to call it a night and stop. I'm $2,100 richer for the price of my soul and body. Juicy thought to herself then pulls out her cellphone and text her best friend Marvin.

'I'm so ready to go home but I just can't seem to tell my sisters no.' Juicy texts and presses send.

Marvin read the text and shook his head and began to text. *'Juicy you're a grown ass woman. I understand times are hard but you don't have to sell your body if you truly don't want too. You can just stand up to your sister and tell her no.'* Marvin wrote and presses send.

Juicy read the text and sighs out of stress, then texts. *'You just don't understand. I can never tell Tatiana no, she did more for me in my life than anyone.'* Juicy wrote and presses send as her mind flashes back to when she was twelve years old and Tatiana was fourteen years old. Their mother had just left to go to work, leaving them in the house with Dustin, like she had done for years.

Dustin busts open the room door with a sick twisted smile on his face that Juicy and Tatiana had seen all too many times. They sat on their beds trembling in fear as he stood in the doorway, only wearing a dirty pair of boxer briefs. His skinny brown body frame looked like it belonged to a scarecrow. He stuck his skinny hand into his boxer briefs and began to play with himself.

You two know what to do, I shouldn't have to keep telling you what to do by now, start fucking kissing already! Dustin shouted then smiled, showing off his yellow stained teeth.

Juicy's little facial expression balls up as she was getting ready to cry.

Shhhh, don't cry Juicy, I will take care of us. We don't need mommy or anyone else. Tatiana said as she looks at her sister and wipes her tears away.

It hurts Tatiana; I don't want him hurting me anymore. Juicy replied with tears in her voice, sounding as if she just wanted to break down crying hysterically.

FETISH

Shhhh! Tatiana said as their lips locked and then kiss one another deeply and passionately.

That's what I'm talking about. You both were doing way to much damn talking for my taste. Dustin said as he continues to jerk his dick back and forth in his boxer briefs, then pulls down his briefs and walks toward them with lust in his eyes as he watch their hands roam over each other's young bodies.

No one loves you two but me. Not even your mother care about you. You think she don't know what we do. Of course she does, it's been going on for three years. She just doesn't care about y'all and love me more. Dustin said as he broke the girls embrace and rips off Juicy nightgown.

He always started with her first, she was his favorite. There was something about her innocent ways and tears that turn him on.

You just don't move and wait until it's your turn. Dustin said to Tatiana as he forces himself inside of Juicy.

Noooo! Ugghhh! Juicy cried and tries to ignore the pain, but that was impossible to

166

do with him long thrusting in and out of her womb.

Tatiana eases off the bed. Juicy turns her head and their eyes met. Juicy mouths the words. Please dont leave me Tatiana. With tears streaming down her face. *'Shhhh I'll be back, stay strong little sister.'* Tatiana mouths the words back. She looks at Juicy one more time before slowly tip-toes away.

Dustin was too deep into what he was doing that with his loud grunting he didnt notice or hear her. His grunting sounds and Juicy crying could be heard echoing throughout the small apartment.

Tatiana made her way to her mothers room that smelled of hot sweaty feet mixed with sex. Tatiana smiled because usually her mothers room door was locked to keep her and Juicy out of the room in fear they will steal money and run away and tell someone whats been going on in their household. Another reason for keeping the door locked was so that Juicy and Tatiana couldnt get their hands on the only phone in the house, but with Dustin being the horny old pervert that he was, he had forgotten to lock the door.

FETISH

Tatiana tip-toes over the dirty clothes on the room floor and grabbed the black house phone on the nightstand. She quickly dials 911.

"Hello this is 911 what is your emergency?"An operator said.

"Hi I'm Tatiana and I'm thirteen years old and my address is 323 Southern Blvd, Apartment 3C. My mother's boyfriend rapes me and my younger sister Juicy. He's been doing it for three years now, he's raping my sister now and I'm next, I'm sneaking to make this call. Please send help. I'll leave the front door unlocked. You will be able to hear our screams and cries for help."Tatiana said in a whisper.

"Wait! Stay on the line until the police officers arrive."The operator responded.

"No I can't, just send help now before it is too late." Tatiana said and hangs up the phone.

She swiftly tip-toes out of the room and shuts the door. She could still hear Dustin grunting and Juicy crying letting her know Dustin hasn't noticed her missing as yet. She crept back in the room and sits on the floor just as Dustin pulls out of Juicy. Juicy crawls up into a ball while laying naked and crying.

Now get your ass up and on the bed and let's get started! He shouted while looking at Tatiana.

Her facial expression balls up with anger mixed with sadness as she gets up off the floor and climbs onto the bed. She then slowly removes the blue nightgown over her head. Dustin wasted no time to attack her, ripping her panties off and climbing on top of her, forcing her legs apart and pushes himself inside her. She learned to hold her tears in, knowing that he seeing her cry only turned him on even more. It was one of the many reasons Juicy was his favorite.

You think you're tough? You always do, but your ass always breakdown and cry at the end. Dustin said with a twisted sick look on his face as he thrusts in and out of her.

She grips his back, digging her little nails into his flesh, her facial expression balls up in pain and she wanted to scream. Tears started to seek out the corner of her eyes. She heard a noise over Dustin's loud grunting and Juicy's crying. She leans her head to the side to look behind Dustin who was on top of her to see two police officers push open the front door of the apartment that she had left cracked.

"Is anybody here, Police?" One officer shouted as he knocks on the open door.

"Ahhhh! Ahhhh! Help me! No stop, you're hurting me! Take it out, take it out! Ahhhh! Ahhhh!" Tatiana screamed at the top of her lungs.

Dustin looks down at her and became immensely excited.

"Oh yes, I knew your ass would break!" Dustin shouted.

From the front door the police officers could make out what was happening in the back bedroom down the hallway. Once they heard Tatiana screams and cries for help they drew their weapons and ran towards the back room. They froze in shock as they saw Juicy naked on one of the twin size beds in the room crying and crawled up into a ball. Then they see a grown brown skin complexion skinny frame man humping in and out of a small child.

⌐Freeze, put your fucking hands up you sick bastard!⌐ One of the police officers shouted.

Dustin⌐s heart raced from the booming sound of the police officer⌐s voice. He knew he was caught off guard. He looks down at Tatiana⌐s face as tears stream down her cheeks, but had a huge Kool-Aid smile on her face showing off her white teeth.

⌐You did this you little bitch. I⌐ll get you for crossing me, I swear!⌐ He said with a deranged look in his eyes.

He quickly slides out of her and grabs Juicy in one swift move putting her in a headlock using her as a shield. Juicy cried out with a confused look on her face not knowing what he was going to do. All she saw were guns pointed at her and Dustin. His arm grips tightly around her little neck.

⌐Juicy, look at this shit on YouTube, it⌐s funny as hell.⌐Tatiana said snapping Juicy out of her flashback.

Juicy looked down at her iPhone reading the text message from her best friend Marvin once more.

'*You will never truly understand why I can never say no to my sister. She's my saver.*' Juicy wrote then presses send.

⬜Yo Juicy, just look at this shit and stop texting for a second.⬜ Tatiana said while pushing her Samsung Galaxy Android phone into Juicy⬜s hands.

Juicy⬜s eyes lit up as she looks at the touch screen at the YouTube video at a fat dark skinned man with braids in his hair, only wearing tight white boxers running down the street with a man wearing a leather sex mask, with a spike collar around his neck and dressed in all black with a paddle that had spikes on it, smacking the fat man on the ass as he screams for help. The man ran up to a few cars that had stopped in the street just to watch what was going on. The people inside their cars pulled out their cell phones and began recording everything while laughing and keeping their doors locked until the man in the leather sex mask killed one of the drivers with the paddle then smashes open the head of the fat man with braids in his hair.

⬜Ahhhh! Is this real or fake?⬜ Juicy asked in horror passing her sister back the phone.

I don't think it's real, but there's four more videos up on YouTube recorded by different people, so it could be real. Tatiana said while laughing.

That's funny Tatiana? If it is real you're sick. You didn't think that guy looked familiar, like one of those four men from our last date? Juicy asked.

Tatiana shook her head no. Most men look the same to me. All I see is a dollar sign, that's my only concern and should be yours as well. Tatiana replied.

Everything in life isn't always about a dollar sign. Juicy responded.

Let you tell it. That's a saying broke people say. Just get out the car so we can do this date. These guys will be like the last ones. No freaky fetishes, they're cheap so it's just a hundred dollars for a half hour then we're out like Jay-Z said on to the next one.

The door opens up and a handsome brown skin complexion man with a New York snap back hat was standing there with a cheese smile on his face.

⌐Hey Tatiana boo.⌐ He said in a deep voice and moves to the side and lets them in.

'Damn, he is a fine ass sexy man. I hope he has a big dick, my pussy just got moist by just looking at him. He'll be the first one out of all the dates I actually do want to fuck.' Juicy thought to herself.

⌐Hey Zavion!⌐ Tatiana said as she enters the house.

⌐Hmmm, and who might this be? You told me you had a friend for my boy, Tatiana.⌐ He said with lust in his eyes. ⌐But you didn⌐t tell me she was so fine.⌐ Zavion said as he stares at Juicy with lust in his eyes, causing her to blush.

Tatiana was 5⌐6⌐ tall with a beautiful face and skin complexion of honey. She was far from skinny, thick in all the right places, but compared to Juicy she looked regular. Juicy was 5⌐3⌐ tall with a dark brown skin complexion, with full luscious lips. Hips that poked out and an ass you could set a cup on. She had a little gut, making her stomach poke out from eating, but you could barely notice it because the way her body filled out. What attracted men to her was the innocent look on her face, like a child but yet you could tell she was a freak.

⬜Thats my sister. I brought her for your friend.⬜Tatiana said as she got up in his face and licks her lips seductively trying to take his mind off of Juicy.

'I don't know why niggas always fall head over heels for her ass when I'm the better fuck and bitch. I'll be damn if I let her steal any of my main customers away.' Tatiana thought to herself as she felt slightly jealous.

Zavion looks at Tatiana and felt his dick rise to the account.

⬜Oh yea, my boy is in the bedroom stressed out over some girl. You and I will do us in the living room and they can do them in there.⬜ Zavion said while pointing to the bedroom door.

⬜Thats cool with me. Juicy go to the bedroom.⬜Tatiana ordered.

⬜I have to go by myself?⬜ Juicy responded with a petrified look on her face.

Tatiana shook her head and walks over to her and whispers into her ear.

"Bitch, get your ass in that room and get that money, nothing's going to happen to you. Stop acting so scared and childish all the time. I have your back."

Juicy sighs and looks at her sister then walks toward the bedroom. Zavion watches her thick voluptuous ass switch in her pink dress as she walks.

"Ummmm, I'm right here." Tatiana said grabbing his chin and turning his head around to face her.

She slips out her skin tight jeans and takes off her shirt, then steps back into her high heels and stood there with her hands on her hips acting as if she was posing for a picture. Zavion licks his lips and walks over to her and palm her ass, while she unbuttons his belt and pulls down his jeans. She then spits on her hand and strokes his dick back and forth.

"Mmmm!" He groans from the sweet tender touch of her little soft hand.

He looks down as she got onto her knees and takes him into her mouth.

FETISH

Juicy nervously opens the room door and looks back at her sister giving Zavion a blow job.

'Dammit, why couldn't I have him?' She thought to herself as she steps into the room and shuts the door.

The room was dim, only a lamp on a nightstand was on. A thick grey cloud of weed smoke covers the room like a blanket. Juicy uses her hand to fan the smoke out of her face and could see a Caucasian man sitting on the edge of the bed with a black hoodie on and blue jeans. Juicy smiles as she studies his face.

'Damn he's a cutie and looks like a young Eminem with brown hair and blue eyes.' Juicy thought to herself.

Hi I'm Juicy. She said.

I'm Jerry-F and I'm a little wasted. He immediately said.

Were you drinking? Juicy asked.

No, I been smoking sour diesel weed all night and I had some coke. Jerry-F replied then pulls out a small baggie of cocaine.

"Do you mind?" He asks.

"No, do whatever makes you feel comfortable, as long as you don't freak out on me." Juicy replied.

"Do you want some?" He offers as he sprinkles some coke onto the nightstand and snorts it up with a rolled up dollar bill.

"No thank you." Juicy said trying to turn him down politely.

"I just broke up with my girlfriend. I caught her fucking one of my best friends. I'm trying to cope with it. Can you play some rap music?" Jerry-F says.

Juicy looks at him then pulls out her cell phone and could see she had another text message from Marvin. She ignores it and went straight into her music playlist and puts on Drake and Eminem's new song.

Jerry-F lay back on the bed then pulls down his jeans and boxers. Juicy pulled out a condom from her purse and sat down on the bed next to him.

"Oh my God!" She said out loud and covers her mouth as she stares at his dick.

FETISH

'This must be the world's smallest penis.' She thought to herself as she continues to stare at his dick that looks more like a skinny thumb.

Come on let's get started. Jerry-F said.

Juicy rips open the condom and tries to roll it on, but it wouldn't fit. She tried three more times with no luck.

Damn! She said out loud then puts the condom into her mouth and began to give him a blow job, sucking his dick and working the condom onto it at the same time.

'Dammit get hard already.' She said to herself as she became frustrated that she had been sucking his dick for a half hour and he still wasn't hard yet.

Juicy sighs in relief when his little dick finally stood up straight.

Let's fuck. He said in a hyped tone as he climbs on top of her.

She removes her thong as he push her legs up and slides inside her and pounds away.

'*Oh my God, I can't feel anything his thighs hitting against mine.*' She thought to herself as she changes positions to doggy style, but his dick was soft and numb, even for a penis.

He pounds away furiously and all she felt were his thighs hitting against her ass cheeks.

Oh man it went down again, it must be the coke. Jerry-F said as he pulls out of her.

I never knew it was up. Juicy said up under her breath. Do you want me to give you another blow job? She asks.

No I'm good it probably won't even get up. I'm high as a kite right now. He said then jumps off the bed and gets dressed then passes her two hundred dollars.

Can we just sit here and talk? Jerry-F asks.

Sure I guess so, why not. Juicy replied.

After listening to him talk about his ex-girlfriend for another half hour. She decided she had heard enough.

⌐Okay I have to go.⌐ Juicy said while leaving him snorting more cocaine off the nightstand and still talking non-stop and never notices her walking away and leaving the room shutting the door behind her.

'I hope I don't interrupt Tatiana and that fine handsome Zavion.' Juicy thought to herself, but was shocked to see them on the couch smoking a blunt and talking.

⌐How did it go in there?⌐Tatiana asked as she sees Juicy approach them.

Juicy looked at Zavion before answering.

'I'll tell you about the world's smallest penis ever later after we leave here.' Juicy thought to herself.

⌐It went okay.⌐ Juicy replied while looking at Zavion staring at her as if she was something to eat.

Juicy couldn⌐ help but to blush. Zavion leans over and whispers into Tatiana⌐ ear.

⌐Schmmp!⌐Tatiana sucks her teeth and her facial expression twists up.

"Okay give me the damn money." She said with an attitude and stuck out her hand.

Zavion digs in his pocket and pulls out a hundred dollar bill and passes it to her. Tatiana quickly stuffs it into her purse with her facial expression twisted up in anger.

Zavion stood up off the black couch and walks over to Juicy. He gently grabs her hand and spins her around slowly looking at her thighs and ass.

"Hmmm, damn you sexy. Come with me baby doll." He said.

"What? Where?" Juicy asked then looks at her sister.

"Just go with him, he paid for a quickie." Tatiana said with an attitude.

"Really?" Juicy said with a huge smile on her face.

A part of her was excited. Zavion was tall and sexy, with a handsome face and a nice brown skin complexion she loved on a man.

'God I hope he has a big dig dick and fucks me good after what just happen in the room and seeing the world's smallest penis. I *could use some good dick.'* Juicy thought to herself as she was lead into the bathroom.

'Ewww!' She said as she looks around the bathroom that looked like a man owned it and it wasn't clean at all.

'You're way prettier and sexier than your sister, I wanted you as soon as I laid my eyes on you, but had to please Tatiana's ass first so she wouldn't get too jealous when I made my move.' Zavion said as he made Juicy arch her back and bend over.

She held on to the dirty sink as he lifts up her pink dress and was pleased to see that she had on no panties. He works on the condom and eases himself inside her, inch by inch.

'Shiiit! Ahhhh shit!' Juicy moans. *'Yes this nigga got a big ass dick, just what I needed and he hasn't even gotten it all the way inside me yet and it's touching my walls. I hope he fucks the shit out of me.'* Juicy thought to herself.

'Ohhhh yesss!' She moans as he works his manhood in and out of her wet pussy.

Zavion held tight on her waist. Then he thrusts in and out of her fast like a jack rabbit.

Ugghhh! Yes, fucking yes! He grunted then stops as he climaxes coming inside the condom and stops moving while breathing hard. Then his body shook a few times then he pulls out of her.

Damn that was great. Zavion said while still breathing hard.

What the fuck just happened! Juicy shouted with a puzzled confused look on her face.

I just nut, that pussy was the bomb.

Zavion you're not serious? Really, ten seconds of fast pumping like a little puppy in heat and you're done? Juicy asked as she couldn't believe what just had happened even knowing she seen it with her own eyes.

Yea that's it for now, I have to wait an hour before I can get it back up and do that again. Zavion replied.

Juicy blinks her eyes a few times with a dumb look on her face. She pulls down her dress and left the bathroom and could see Tatiana sitting on the couch still smoking a blunt with a big smile on her face already knowing what her sister had experienced.

ꞏCome on lets go, we got more money to chase.□Tatiana said as they left the small apartment.

ꞏYou knew he had a big dick and didnꞏt know how to work it, didnꞏt you?□He came in ten seconds.□ Juicy said as they left the building and hops into Tatianaꞏs grey Mercedes Benz.

ꞏYea I knew, but look what you made for that ten seconds of humping, a hundred dollars like it was nothing. Oh yea you need to give me a cut of the money from the dude in the bedroom. How was he anyway? You were in there for like an hour.□Tatiana said as she pulls off.

ꞏAll I can say is he looked like Eminem, but cried like a girl over his ex and had the worldꞏs smallest penis.□Juicy replied causing Tatiana to bust out laughing as she drove down the block.

Chapter 11

The Stalker watches their car pull off. Hate mixed with rage consumes his body.

'Why do they have to keep doing this?' He said out loud to himself as he grabs the leather sex mask and paddle from the back seat and steps out of his car looking both ways making sure no one was out as he enters the building and went straight to the second floor.

He slides the leather sex mask on his face and zips it up in the back. Then he zips the mouth piece close. He knocks on the door while pressing his thumb on to the peephole of the door.

Who is it? Zavion said and looks through the peephole, but only could see a black spot.

Who is it? Zavion shouted as the knocking continues and he couldn't see anything and gets no reply.

It's probably Tatiana's ass coming back to give me a freebie. Hahahaha! Zavion said while laughing and opens the door and wishes he hadn't, as he came face to face with a weird looking man with a leather sex mask on.

What the fuck is this. I know its Halloween time, but we're grown. I don't have time for trick or treat! Zavion shouted.

The Stalker smiled behind the leather sex mask and raises his hand pressing the Taser against Zavion's throat.

Ugghha! Ugghha! Zavion screams as 500 volts travel through his body and he foams at the mouth as his eyes rolls into the back of his head.

I don't want you dying too fast big fella. The Stalker said and removes the Taser from Zavion's neck and watches Zavion fall backwards while shaking on the floor and looks as if he was going into convulsions. The Stalker unzips his mouth piece on the leather sex mask and walks into the apartment and shuts the door behind him.

You went down fast big guy. It's true the bigger you are the harder you fall. The Stalker said as he bends over and removes Zavion's boots then his clothes.

A sound from the bedroom startled him making him freeze in his tracks as he removes Zavion's shirt. The Stalker stood up straight and walks to the bedroom. He turns the doorknob and pushes open the door to see a Caucasian man that looks to be no more than twenty-two. He was sitting on the edge of the bed snorting coke off the nightstand and smoking a blunt at the same time.

Did anyone ever tell you that you look just like Eminem? The Stalker said as he stared at the young man.

Jerry-F took a deep pull of the blunt and looks at him. His eye lids were low and his face was bright red. The Stalker could tell he was beyond high and it was causing his brain to think slowly.

Yea my ex used to tell me that all the time before I caught her cheating on me with one of my best friends. That shit got me really messed up in the head. I must be to high dude do you have a mask on your face? Jerry-F said with his words slurred as he shook his head from side to side and wipes the cocaine from his nose.

The Stalker walks up to him and swung the paddle knocking him in the jaw.

Ugghhh! Jerry-F groan in pain as blood gushes out his mouth.

FETISH

The Stalker grabs him by the leg and drags him off the bed.

"Ahhhh! Nooo! What's going on? Why are you doing this dude? Please stop! Ahhhh!" Jerry-F cried out.

The Stalker stared at him with evil rage in his eyes.

"It's because you touched what belongs to me. Those women that were in here a few minutes ago are mine. And you're supposed to kill who ever touch what's yours. If you were a real man, that's what you would've done when you caught your woman fucking your best friend!"The Stalker shouted.

"I didn't even do anything with her, please!" Jerry-F shouted as he gets dragged from the bedroom.

His low eye lids opens up wide in horror as the paddle covered in metal spikes came crashing down on his face.

"Ahhhh! Ahhhh! Ahhhh!"He hollered in pain as every bone in his face shatters and mushes in.

He chokes on five of his front teeth as they broke off and went down his throat. The

Stalker stops and looks on in amazement. Jerry-F's face had been completely smashed in, blood, bones and the skin of his face was everywhere, but yet Jerry⬛F was still moving and trying to talk. The Stalker pulls out his cellphone from his pocket and starts recording.

⬛ got this idea from the teenager's I killed not too long ago. They put me on YouTube smashing in a fat prick face like I did yours. It was a great video, but I think they caught my bad side making me look fat. I'll do better recording for myself.☐ He said with a twisted sick smile on his face as he licks his lips.

Zavion finally stops shaking and regains consciousness. He turns around onto his back and realizes he was stripped naked. He tilts his head to the left and looks over in terror at a man dressed in all-black with a leather sex mask on his face and a phone in his left hand and a paddle covered in small melt spikes that was dripping dark red blood onto the floor. Zavion looks down to see what the Stalker was recording.

⬛Ahhhh! Ahhhh!☐ He screams, but quickly covers his mouth to keep the screams from being too loud as he looks at his friend whose face had been pounded in.

Blood was leaking everywhere and yet his lips were still moving and his body was twitching, shaking up and down on the floor. Zavion quietly eases off the floor without making a sound.

Zavion was six feet tall and 170 pounds. He outweighed the Stalker and was about the same height. The Stalker had a skinny twisted scary body frame like a scarecrow.

'I can take him, I can take him.' Zavion repeatedly said in his head to hype himself and build his confidence.

⌐Ahhhh! Ahhhh!☐He screams letting out a war cry as he charges the Stalker.

The Stalker turns his head from hearing the loud scream, before he could react a right hook to the face caught him off guard making him stumble backwards as he receives two more punches too the face.

⌐Uggghhh!☐The Stalker groans in pain as he tries to catch his balance.

⌐Ahahahah!☐Zavion let out another war cry and swung with all his might with an upper cut punch, that sent the Stalker straight up into the air and he hits the floor hard lying on his back, dropping the leather paddle that was covered in spikes and blood.

"You motherfucker, you want to come in my apartment and attack me? I'll kill you! I'll kill your ass!" Zavion hollered as he sent blow after blow to the Stalker's face.

"Ugghhaaa!" The Stalker groans in pain from each hit.

All he could see was stars and the color black and blue from his head spinning.

"I'll teach you, you damn freak. Let's see who's behind this freaky looking sex mask!" Zavion shouted then rips the mask off the Stalker's face.

Zavion froze as his heart races and fear consumes his body. His hands shook and stomach bubbles as he felt as if he was about to move his bowels and shit on himself. He stared at the Stalker then screams.

"Ahhhh! Ahhhh! Ahhhh!" In a high pitch tone that you would swear came from a woman.

The Stalker had no skin on his face at all as if it all had been peeled off or burned off by a blowtorch. He had no eyelids and a thin piece of meat no one in their right mind would call lips. It gave the illusion that he was smiling. The Stalker stares back at Zavion with his big eyes that stood red because he had no eyelids to blink. The Stalker buckles his body, knocking Zavion off him. All the courage in Zavion he once had escaped his heart as he crawls backwards on the floor still staring at the Stalker's horrifying face.

⌐Ahhhh! Ahhhh!⌐ He screams as his hand touches what was left of his friend's forehead and he could still see his body twitching.

⌐Ahhhh! What the fuck are you man?⌐ Zavion screams as tears roll down his cheek.

The Stalker stood up straight and picks up the leather sex mask and slides it back on to his face, zipping it up.

⌐Ahhhh! Noooo! Stay away from me! Ahhhh!⌐Zavion screamed and pops up off the floor and runs into the bedroom.

He twists the small lock on the door locking the door behind him. He then pushes the queen size bed against the door. His heart beats fast and his palms were dripping of sweat as he back pedals and looks at the doorknob shake as the Stalker tries to get in.

Then he could hear banging as the Stalker throws himself up against the door in rage. He stops and swings the paddle hard three times, knocking the doorknob off the door and then pushes the door. The queen size bed was firm against the door it slows him down, but did little to stop him. Seeing that the Stalker was almost through the door Zavion began to panic and look around the room for something he could use as a weapon. He then looks at the window behind him.

'Oh shit I'm a dumb ass. I can climb out the window and go down the fire escape.' He said out loud to himself.

He ran to the window and moves the curtains to the side while continuing to turn his head looking at the door open inch by inch as the Stalker pushes the bed away from the door. Terror consumes Zavions body as he tries to open up the window but his palms were sweating profusely.

Yes! He shouted in excitement as he opens the window.

FETISH

He looks behind himself in horror as he could see half the Stalker's body squeezing through the door and he was now staring at him.

"Ahhhh!" Zavion screams as he climbs out the window head first in a rush to escape the apartment.

The Stalker raises his left hand with the paddle in it and throws the paddle with all his might. It hits the window shattering glass everywhere making the window frame fall on top of Zavion's neck.

"Euggghhh!" He made a gagging sound and tries to lift the window frame up off his neck, but it was stuck after being broken. The Stalker squeezes through the door and enters room with a smile on his face as he look at Zavion's naked body flopping around like a fish out of water as he struggles to get the window frame off his neck, but it went in vain as he steps on pieces of glass that went deep into his bare feet.

The Stalker took his phone out of his pocket and sits it up straight on the night stand. He presses record then looks at the screen making sure it was in the right angle.

FETISH

⌐Stupid motherfucker, you were in such a rush to escape you didn⌐t think to put your feet out the window first before your head, you idiot!⌐The Stalker said then laughs.

⌐I⌐m going to have a fun with you just like you did with Juicy and Tatiana.⌐ The Stalker said as he picks up a piece of the shattered glass from the floor by Zavion⌐s feet.

⌐No! Stay the fuck away from me man! Help! Help me! Please don⌐t kill me. I was only with them both for ten minutes, I have a problem I cum fast and can⌐t even get hard for like an hour, I swear!⌐Zavion screamed while crying.

⌐Hahahaha, that⌐s too bad for you, that ten minutes of pleasure will be the reason your life ends tonight, don⌐t worry it won⌐t take me no longer than five minutes to finish you off.⌐ The Stalker replied.

⌐Noooo!⌐Zavion hollered as the Stalker spreads his ass cheeks apart and forces the broken piece of glass into his anal.

The Stalker held the piece of glass with one hand and the paddle with the other and swung it. Hitting the glass like a hammer and nail, forcing it deeper into Zavion⌐s ass.

'Ahhhh! Ahhhh! Ahhhh!' Zavion screamed while crying.

Soon the piece of glass was stuck far into his anal. The Stalker no longer had to hold it with his left hand. He turns around to face his cellphone on the nightstand that was recording everything and he smiled.

'God, uggghhh, help me! Help me! I'm sorry!' Zavion hollered.

An elderly woman in the building across from Zavion looks out her window to see what was going on and what all the noise was about.

'Who in the hell is making all that noise this late at night?' She said to herself as she moves her curtains to get a better view of the building next to hers.

'Oh my!' She said out loud startled as she looks at Zavion with his head out the window and the other half of his body inside his apartment, then sees a man in a leather sex mask and a paddle in his hand.

The Stalker looks up and smiles then waves hi and went back to swinging the paddle hitting the glass deeper into Zavion's ass as if he was hammering a nail into the wall.

"Oh my, these young people get worse and worse. What kind of freaky devil stuff is that? They need Jesus in their lives. Oh Lord." The elderly woman said as she felt she has seen way too much for her old eyes and closed her curtains shut and grabs her bible and start reading.

Whack! Whack! Whack! The sound of the paddle echoed with each blow the Stalker made.

"Aaaaahhhh!" Zavion screams in excruciating pain as the piece of glass went all the way up into his anal as if his asshole just swallowed it.

"Ahhhh, please stop! No more! Noooo!" Zavion hollered as The Stalker picks up another piece of shattered glass from the floor, even longer.

He grins with a sick twisted smile. The smell of feces and urine mixed with blood was strong in the air. As Zavion hollered in agonizing pain and felt as if he was going to pass out. He tries to force out the glass that was already stuck inside his anal but shitted on himself.

FETISH

"Ewww, you're a nasty bastard!" The Stalker shouted and went back to work banging the long piece of glass inside his anal.

"Help me! Help me!" Zavion screamed.

"Whack! Whack! Whack! Whack!" The sound of the paddle made with each blow.

The long piece of glass went deeper and deeper, ripping and tearing up internal organs.

"Uggghhh!" Zavion hollered one last excruciating scream as blood oozes out of his mouth and anal and his body twitches and he dies.

The Stalker looks down at Zavion's naked body in disgust. Feces were on the floor mixed with blood a piece of glass was still hanging out of his ass.

"Motherfucker, that's for messing with what is mine." The Stalker said then left the bedroom, walking over Jerry-F's body as he enters the bathroom.

He washed the blood and feces off the paddle and his hands then grab his cellphone off the nightstand in the room and left the building.

ꞏLetꞏs see what they think of this.ꞏThe Stalker said as he sat in his car and uploads the recorded video to YouTube then started up the car and pulls off.

Chapter 12

ꞏMmmm.ꞏJuicy moans in her sleep as the smell of bacon and eggs with grits hit her nose. *'I love that fact my sister always cooks in the morning.*ꞏShe said to herself as she sat up in her bed only wearing a pink nightgown. ꞏDamn that food smells good. Tatiana is doing her thing in the kitchen.ꞏ Juicy said as she pulls out her cellphone from up under her pillow and reads the time, 8:00 am. *'Damn where does she get the energy from, we didn't get home until five this morning.'* Juicy thought to herself as she eases out of her bed.

⌐Ouch! Damn it! My pussy is still sore.⌐ She said out loud as she took baby steps out of her room.

Each step hurt more than the last. She felt as if it took her forever to make it inside the bathroom in the hallway. She gets undressed and hops in the shower and lets the hot water ease her body.

⌐Ouch!⌐ She groans as she places her hand with the wash cloth in between her legs.

Tears stream down her face as flashbacks of all the men she slept with played in her mind.

'Damn, I wish I could be strong enough to tell Tatiana no.' Juicy said out loud to herself as she finished washing up and gets out the shower. She dries her body off and walks back to her room happy that the hot shower had somewhat helped the soreness between her legs.

She pulled out a Rocawear pink sweat suit and made her way downstairs to the kitchen and was surprised to see Kandy-Cola dressed in a white silk robe and Shanelle in a black teddy eating at the table while Tatiana stood over the stove finishing up cooking the bacon.

Good morning Ms. Innocent, I heard you finally popped that cherry and decided to use your inner freakiness to get some real money and join the team, hahaha. Kandy-Cola said in a playful manor while laughing and causing Tatiana and Shanelle to laugh as well.

Shut up! I had no choice. I got fired from my job and was short on my share of rent. Juicy said then smiles.

She hated Shanelle and Kandy-Colas smart sarcastic mouths, but loved them like sisters she never had.

Well that shit paid off, because you made close to four thousand dollars last night. Money that would ve taken you three or four months to make at that bullshit security guard job you had. Tatiana said as she walks over to the dining room table and places a plate of food in front of her sister.

Juicy looks at the bacon and eggs with girts with cheese and a smile spread across her face as she picks up her fork and digs in.

Damn Juicy's making more money than me now! That shit is just sad. Shanelle said as she stuffs a piece of bacon in her mouth as Tatiana sat down at the table with her plate and joins them.

Everybody is making more money than you. It's time you gave up on that abortion hustle. I don't see how that shit is still working. Most niggas know that game and tell your ass to get on Medicaid, I keep telling you that. Aren't you suppose to fake getting pregnant not really get knock up though? Kandy-Cola said in a sarcastic tone then laughs.

Shanelle squint her eyes and stares at her with hate and jealousy in them.

Well we all can't be like you and get rappers and entertainers to take care of us. If you didn't have that body of yours you wouldn't be able to pull them. Shanelle spit out.

Schmmp! Bitch please, with this body or not, I would still pull them. It's all about your game and holding out for these thirsty niggas. Make them beg for it then turn them the fuck out. You can pull the same men I do. You're a sexy slim bitch, with long weave and look like a beautiful black Barbie doll with a fat ass. The difference between us is that I use my game and refuse to settle for less than the best." Kandy-Cola said with a smirk on her face and continues eating her food.

"Shanelle don't pay her any mind, at least you're not one of those broke chicks who don't do anything with their lives you're getting money." Tatiana said cooling the situation down, because all of them knew how bad Shanelle was when she got started.

There was no stopping her and she could get louder than most ghetto chick heads from the projects.

"Nah, I'm good Kandy, it's not getting to me she's just acting fancy because she became Casino-Rich's main lady." Shanelle replied.

"Word bitch, you're Casino-Rich's woman now and you didn't tell me, and you actually let a man lock you down. That never happened out of all the years I've known you." Tatiana stated.

FETISH

Kandy-Cola just stares at Shanelle as if she wanted to slap her.

Shanelle smiled. "What, they were going to find out, the shits all over the radio and Facebook, plus Twitter. That and the shootout at Club Perfections, four people was killed and seven others were shot." Shanelle said.

Tatiana looks at Twitter on her iPhone. "Oh shit and you wasn't going to tell us. So does that mean you're moving and going to live with your new hubby?" Tatiana said.

"Hahahaha, I was going to tell y'all, but I'm still working him over and locking his ass down, and hell no I'm never leaving you bitches. I love my girls even Shanelle's smart ass mouth." Kandy-Cola replied.

"Awwww, we love you too Tatiana." Juicy and Shanelle said simultaneously.

"That fool Casino-Rich gave me an offer I couldn't refuse, fifty thousand a month to be his woman. You know I said hell to the yes, and I'm taking you hoes shopping." Kandy-Cola said.

Fifty thousand a month damn heifer, you done came up in life, we need to hit Manhattan up and shop our butts off.

Ummm! What about Roger? He's not going to like the fact you're claiming a man now when he worked to earn that spot, but you fucking other dudes is one thing, but saying you have a man, Roger's going to have a heart attack. Tatiana said.

Fuck Roger! He's just going have to suck it up and take it, like it or not. Kandy-Cola replied.

I always felt you should be with Roger. He did so much for you and dealt with all your ups and downs and bullshit over the years. That man really loves you. Juicy said.

Tatiana, Shanelle and Kandy-Cola just stared at Juicy as if she lost her mind.

That's your problem Juicy you're too sweet and innocent. Fuck men, it's about money and using them to get what we want. They would use or bodies and cum in them every chance they can get and go on their merry way. I say we use the power between our legs and every time they want to get a taste they have to swipe them debit cards, to hell with love and a free fuck.￼ Kandy-Cola replied.

￼Preach! Amen!￼Tatiana and Shanelle responded simultaneously.

￼Cola! Cola!￼A man screamed loudly, pounding at the front door startling all of them and made their hearts race.

￼Who in the hell is that banging on our front door like the police screaming your name like an insane man.￼ Tatiana said with an attitude.

￼Take one fucking guess. There￼s only one man I know who calls me Cola.￼Kandy-Cola replied as she eases up from her chair and straightens out her silk white robe she had on that did little to hide her perfect shape and left little to the imagination.

￼Well you better get that fool in check out there acting all crazy and shit I￼l bust a cap in his ass.￼Tatiana said with a nasty attitude.

￼Don￼t worry I￼l handle it.￼ Kandy-Cola replied as she made her way to the front door where the loud pounding got even harder.

Kandy-Cola opens up the door to see Roger standing there ready to knock on the door once more. He was dressed in a dark blue suit and his Gucci seeing glasses. Sweat was dripping profusely down his forehead.

What the fuck is your problem Roger! Why are you banging on my door like that and shouting my name! Kandy-Cola shouted with her facial expression twisted up, showing her anger.

How could you do this to me? How Cola? Fucking how? Roger shouted and brushes pass her walking into the house.

Kandy-Cola looks at him.

'Damn you go some nerves walking straight into my place.' She thought to herself. Roger what in the hell are you talking about? Are you high? Kandy-Cola replied.

What am I talking about? What am I talking about? Huh! The shits all over the internet on Facebook and Twitter that your Casino-Rich woman now! How could you do this to me, to us? Roger shouted while moving his hands all around in the air like a crazy person.

Do what to us Roger! The last time I checked I was a grown ass woman and could do what I want. That means see whoever I want and fuck whoever I want, if it be a man or woman! Kandy-Cola said while licking her lips enticing him.

No the hell you cant, not when I invested over 80,000 into your ass. It was cool with you just fucking other men, I didnt mind that at all, but for you to actually claim someone as your man, that hurts! Thats supposed to be my spot and mines only Cola! No one deserves it but me! I love you for who you really are! I wont have this or allow it! Roger shouted with a mixture of rage and love in his eyes.

Kandy you okay? Tatiana asks as she enters the living room and sees Cola standing by the front door.

Stay out of this Tatiana! I blame you for all of this! Before she started hanging with you Cola was never a hoe, you turned her into a slut like the rest of the bitches around you! Roger shouted as he turns and face Tatiana.

You better watch your motherfucking mouth while youre in my house nigga! Dont be mad because a better man done took what you wanted. If you were making real money maybe you wouldnt be feeling so less of a man right now!☐ Tatiana snapped back crushing his heart and ego with her words.

☐I got this Tatiana, just fall back girl.☐ Kandy-Cola said even though she was pissed off at Roger, she didn☐t like anyone bad talking him but herself.

She had love for Roger. He was dealing with her for six years way before the fame and took good care of her until she found men that did the job even better.

☐Alright handle your business then, making all this damn noise nine o☐clock in the morning.☐ Tatiana said as she turns around and leaves the living room.

Roger turns his attention back on Kandy-Cola.

☐So now you☐re just going let your friends disrespect me now?☐Roger said.

☐No Roger, you did that to yourself acting like a lame ass nigga. You need to get out of my house and take your ass to work.☐ Kandy-Cola replied.

☐So it☐s like that? That☐s how you☐re going to do me Cola after all I☐ve done for you? All the money I invested in you, even the

Range Rover out front is in a loan in my name bitch!□Roger shouted.

You repeat yourself a lot. Did anyone ever tell you that?□ Kandy-Cola said and walked out the living room and into her bedroom and returned in the matter of seconds with her cellphone in one hand and a set of keys in the next.

□Here take those!□ She said as she forces the Range Rover keys into the palm of his hand.

□I don□ need that truck anymore! I don□ need or want anything in your name or anything you can use to throw in my face, I□m tired of you repeating yourself and talking about what you□ve done for me. Any dime you spent I will return, you got me a truck on a loan a real man would have gotten me a fully paid for car and wouldn□ keep bringing it up that he did that for me. It would be a small thing to a giant. Let me show you.□Kandy-Cola said as she dials a number on her iPhone and Casino-Rich picks up on the first ring.

□Hey what□s good? What are you doing up so early?□Casino-Rich said.

211

"Good morning Daddy. Now isn't the time to get into all of that, I'll tell you later, but I need a new truck or car, something luxurious and white that matches my swagger. Do you have me?" Kandy-Cola said and presses a button putting the call on speaker.

"Sure, anything for you. We can go pick something out today baby." Casino-Rich replied.

"You're not going to take it out on a loan right?" Kandy-Cola responded.

"I'm a Boss and a Baller, what I look like taking a loan out for any car when I can afford anything I want? What I look like a lame as nigga? Hahahaha!" Casino-Rich said while laughing.

"Okay Daddy, come pick me up at noon, later baby." Kandy-Cola replied.

"Later boo." Casino-Rich said and the phone went dead.

Kandy-Cola stood there with an evil sarcastic smile on her face as she stares at Roger.

"You see the difference from a real man and a lame. I don't need shit from you! I'll send you a check next week for the amount of money you so called invested in me. Now be on your way.☐She said coldly.

Roger held his head down in shame, his body trembles as his heart aches. He felt as if his pride and ego along with his heart had been stomped on repeatedly, and Kandy-Cola squatted down and pissed on it to finish it off. Two tears ran down each of his cheeks. Seeing him cry melts her heart and she knew that she might have gone a little too far.

'Damn I just wanted to make him mad enough that he would forget about me and stop stalking me and acting all crazy.' Kandy-Cola thought to herself.

☐Ahhhh!☐ Roger lifts up his head and looks at the ceiling and then screams with tears rolling down the side of his face and his fist clenched tightly.

☐You think you can just get rid of me that easy! I fucking made you!☐Roger shouted with tears in his voice and charges at her, running at her with full speed.

Kandy-Cola hollered as she was caught off guard also knocking the wind out of here.

"I'll kill you before I let you leave me!" Roger screamed as he sent four punches to her face then jabs her in the eye.

"Ahhhh! Stop! Stop!" Kandy-Cola cried out in pain as she raises her forearms to protect her face the best she could.

"I'll kill you bitch!" Roger shouted as he notices his blows to her face weren't any longer hurting her, because she was using her forearms to protect her face.

"Ugghh! Ahhhh!" She cried out as Roger sent blow after blow to her ribcage.

"Get off my home girl you lame!" Shanelle yelled and hops onto his back, wrapping her arms around his neck choking him.

She opens her mouth wide and sunk her teeth into his shoulder blade.

"Ahhhh! Ahhhh! You skinny, little bitch!" Roger hollered in pain and flips her over his shoulders off his back making her slim body land next to Kandy-Cola.

"It's you bitches fault that she's like this in the first place! We were all good until she decided to leave with y'all four years ago!"

Roger shouted as he stood up straight and began to furiously kick Shanelle in the face and ribs then stomps on Kandy-Cola.

Ugghhaa! Ahhhh! Ahhhh! Both women scream in excruciating pain.

Stop, Roger stop, please! Ahhhh! Kandy-Cola shouted as the heel of his shoe stomped on her right thigh sending agonizing pain through her body.

She rolls around on the floor then crawls up into a ball while holding Shanelle. They both cried out for help as their tears soak the carpet. Something pressing onto the back of Roger's head made him stop his attack. He slowly turns around and looks down to see Tatiana standing in a blue silk robe, with a small chrome .22-Caliber handgun now pointed at his forehead.

Motherfucker if you put your feet on my friends again, treating them like dogs I swear I'll kill you where you stand and I'll get away with it! You're intruding in my house attacking us! Tatiana said through clenched teeth meaning every word.

I expected this shit from one of these thugs or low lives in the street, but not from you

Roger. You're really labeling yourself as a lame weak man putting your hands on women! Tatiana said.

Roger looks down at her, she was only 5'3 tall, but the fire in her eyes was like fire from a giant's eyes. Tears stream down Roger's cheeks. His lips trembles as he spoke.

You did this to her Tatiana. You did it! You broke my heart it's because of you she changed! I don't care kill me you slut! Roger shouted then punches her with a right hook then a left hook to her face, before she knew what happen.

She had fallen to the ground and dropped the gun. All she could see was stars. He drags her next to Kandy-Cola and Shanelle who was hurled up crying while holding each other. Roger began his brutal assassin on all three women.

Ahhhh! Ahhhh! Stop! Please stop! The women cried out in pain as he kicks them then stomps them. When his legs got tired he bends down punching them.

Juicy! Help me! Stop! Stop hitting us! Tatiana screamed.

Juicy couldn't believe her eyes as she watches the brutal attack on her sister and friends and didn't know what to do. She was the most innocent thinking one out of all of them, without a violent bone in her body. Flashbacks of Dustin beating her and Tatiana before raping them played in her mind. She could smell his stink breath of cigarettes as he forced himself inside her. She could feel his boney fingers on her skin.

"Ahhhh! Juicy!" Tatiana screams for help snaps Juicy out of the trance she was in. She grabs a wooden chair from the dining room and lifts it above her head and walks over to Roger who had his back facing her while he took turns kicking the three women. Juicy swung down with the wooden chair with all her strength. The wooden chair came crashing down onto Roger's head and back, breaking into pieces.

"Ugghh!" Roger grunted in pain as he stumbles forward and falls to the ground next to Tatiana.

Juicy quickly picks up the chrome .22-Caliber handgun that fell next to the couch. She aims the gun at him as he held the back of his head rocking back and forth on the floor in pain. Tatiana and Shanelle quickly hop up off the floor and began stomping him.

"You motherfucking little dick nigga, I'll teach you to put your hands on me!" Tatiana shouted as she steps onto his dick with the heel of her foot.

"Ughhh!" Roger screamed.

Kandy-Cola finally hops up off the floor once most the pain in her body had stopped, she balls up her fist and bends over and sends blow after blow to Roger's face. She punches him as if she was a professional boxer.

"Ahhhh! Ahhhh! Ahhhh! Stop! Stop!" Roger hollered as the women kick, stomp and punch him, busting open his skin and lips as blood leaks onto the carpet.

"Juicy get over here and help us fuck this nigga up!" Tatiana shouted out of breath and only stops her attack for a second to look at her sister.

Juicy was in shock and didn't know what to do. She walks over to Roger and lightly kicks him three times in the back.

Harder Juicy, hit that nigga fucking harder or I'm going to beat your ass! Tatiana shouted while kicking Roger in the back.

With the newfound fear of Tatiana beating her ass, Juicy kicks Roger with all her might in the back of his leg over and over. Shanelle drops down on her knees and pounds on him with both her fist wildly.

Motherfucker I'll kill you! She yelled with tears in her eyes.

Ahhhh! Roger hollered in pain.

Get this piece of shit out of my house! Tatiana shouted as they look at Roger badly beaten body.

It took all four of them to drag him by his suit out of the house and leave him on the side walk. Kandy-Cola kicks him in the chin then kicks the skin off his forehead before she walks away. Tatiana snatches the gun out of Juicy's hand.

The next time you come to my door, I won't hesitated on shooting you! Tatiana shouted while pointing the gun at him then walks into the house shutting the door.

"I don't believe that nigga just flipped on me like that and tried to beat the black off me!" Kandy-Cola said while Tatiana sat on the matching black leather loveseat.

"Bitch he wasn't trying to beat the black off you, he was, and whipping our asses along with you. That's the power of the pussy! Make these foolish ass men lovesick and weak then they get crazy after you tell them that they can't have any more. Then this Bitch Juicy was stuck standing in the kitchen like a dear in headlights before the car hits his ass." Tatiana stated.

"Naw, you bugging, my bitch Juicy came through. If it wasn't for her hitting him over the head with that chair Roger would have still been whipping our asses." Shanelle replied.

"Damn it, breaking my good dining room chair, but you did good Juicy. You just have to learn how to react faster if anybody messes with us. We take care of each other, if they're messing with one of us they have to deal with us all!" Tatiana responded.

"Everything happen so fast Tatiana, and it brought my mind back to the past." Juicy replied.

FETISH

Tatiana knew exactly what her sister was talking about, the pain they both shared and now understood why her sister was stuck in a daze.

But we did fuck Roger up! I bet his ass won't be trying that bullshit anymore. Kandy-Cola said while smiling.

Hell yea, I was pounding on his face and back. That bastard fucked up my weave, this that Remy twenty inches, far from cheap. Shanelle replied.

You should get your new boo Casino-Rich to deal with Roger's ass. Tatiana said.

No I can't do that Casino-Rich would have him killed. I think he was behind having the bouncer and other people murdered at the club last night. I'm not even going to tell him about this. Kandy-Cola replied.

So if you're not going to tell him, how are you going to hide that black eye you have. Tatiana said while laughing.

Easy I'll lie and tell him I got into a fight with some hating bitch, which is pretty much the truth, but we need to get ready for the day to go shopping so I can link up with my boo later and get my new ride. Kandy-Cola said.

Ummm, don't y'all think we should call the police and report what just happened? Juicy said in a childlike manner that causes the other three women to bust out laughing.

Hahahaha! Hahahaha! Yo, to be twenty-one Juicy, and from the hood, you're so damn innocent. We don't call the cops in the hood. No one does. I'm pretty sure our neighbors on the block heard us screaming for our lives in this bitch and not one of them called the police. The projects are just up the block from us. All we need is the hustlers to think we're snitching and then we will have more issues, this gun is not even registered. Bitch we are hood. Tatiana said while laughing.

The loud sound of a car alarm made all the women stop their laughter and run to the large living room front window. They could see Roger with his blue suit badly ripped and torn covered in blood. Blood leaked from his face and forehead, his lips were busted. His seeing glasses were missing a lens from the left side and the right side was all twisted up on his face.

FETISH

￼Ahhhh! Ahhhh! I hate you all! I fucking loved you before the famous Cola!￼ Roger shouted as he picks up a rock from off the sidewalk and throws it, breaking the driver￼s side window of the white Rang Rover.

He picks up three more rocks and tosses them breaking the back window and two side windows. He stumbles to his jade green Hummer and pops open the trunk and pulls out a small red container. He stumbled back over to the white Range Rover and pours gas inside through the broken windows and the rest on the other side of the truck. He then lights a match tossing it into the truck. The Range Rover went up in flames as it engulfs in the fire in a matter of seconds.

￼You bitch! I wish I could burn and take everything I ever gotten you! I hate you Cola for letting me love you and using me! I pray everything backfires on you, karma is a bigger bitch than you!￼Roger shouted with tears and blood running down his face as he hops in his truck and pulls off.

￼Damn that man got it bad. Your pussy is good, but not that damn good for him to be acting like that. I know because I taste it all the time.￼Shanelle said with a smirk on her face.

Shut the fuck up! I know how to work my goodie-goods. That's why they go crazy, but Roger is just stupid. The truck is in his name and he just destroyed it and still has to pay the bank back for the loan. He had about $30,000 left to go. I guess we'll be taking your car to go shopping Tatiana. Kandy-Cola said causing all the other women to laugh.

Yea, let's get out of here before the police and fire department show up. Shanelle said as they turned from the window and headed for their rooms.

Shanelle, Kandy-Cola along with Juicy spent most of the day shopping in Manhattan then to the Bronx to buy shoes. As Tatiana pulls her car up on Beach 60 in Far Rockaway, the first thing she noticed was a shiny new black Lamborghini parked in front of her house.

Damn who is that? Tatiana asked as she parks her Mercedes Benz behind the car.

That's my Boo, Casino-Rich. I don't need y'all heifers acting like groupies. I'm about to go with him and pick up my new car. Can y'all please put my bags in my room since I did spend all my money on y'all hoes today? That the least you can do. Kandy-Cola said while texting Casino-Rich on her iPhone.

"So you're just going to flat leave us huh? And we know that's your dick, but you should let us tag along and get with some of those Goonz Squad niggas." Tatiana replied.

"Schmmp! Those niggas are workers, I only associate with bosses, but I'll hook y'all up later I'm still sinking my teeth into Casino-Rich, I have to get him even more open until he can't live without me, then I'll take him for everything he's worth." Kandy-Cola said while sucking her teeth.

"Yea, yea just make it happen, heifer." Tatiana said as Kandy-Cola stuck out her tongue to her and gets out the car and shuts the door and seductively walks over to the black Lamborghini.

"Her and her conceited ass, I got something she can do with that tongue of her. Let's get all the bags out of my car and into the house. I got money for us to make." Tatiana stated.

"Again, didn't we make enough money last night Tati, and my good-good is still a little sore?" Juicy responded, causing Tatiana to turn around and look at her in the back seat.

She and Shanelle both stared at Juicy.

"Juicy I swear you say the stupidest things sometimes or sound like a child. There's no such thing as making enough or too much money. Jump your ass in the shower, soak that pussy and get ready for tonight." Tatiana replied.

Juicy held her head down. *'Why she can't understand I don't want to do this, my body shouldn't have a price tag on it and sold to the highest bidder.'* Juicy thought to herself.

"Shanelle do you want to roll with us tonight, I need an extra girl and it's been a while since you've gotten your abortion? So are you in, the pay will be good? Tatiana said.

"Hell yea I'm down! The day that Juicy booty over there starts making more money than me is time to switch the hustle."Shanelle replied while grabbing some of the shopping bags from floor of the car and Juicy did the same.

The Lamborghini's passenger side door cut up into the air as it opens up. Kandy-Cola got in and shuts the door.

"Mmmm!"She let out a slight moan and couldn't help but to become moist between her legs as she looks at Casino-Rich.

His dreads were freshly twisted that stopped at his shoulders. He had crusted diamond earrings in both his ears. The famous Goonz Squad medallion with an eagle encrusted on a green diamond chain was around his neck. He had on a black Gucci T-shirt with the matching jeans and a thick diamond bracelet that covered his entire wrist. Casino-Rich turns his head and his eyes rested on Kandy-Cola's thick voluptuous brown skin thighs that were showing off in a short white channel dress she had on. Then he studies her face and could see the bruise and wondered why she had on a pair of dark Prada glasses when it was cloudy outside.

Take the glasses off I want to see your eyes. Casino-Rich said.

She slowly removes her Prada sunglasses.

Damn, what happen to you baby? Who in the hell put their hands on my woman? I'll kill them! He said meaning every word as he stares at her black eye.

It's nothing Daddy, just a few bitches hating on me. One of them sucker punched me and I can't front she got me good, but me and my girls handled their asses and whipped those hoes to the ground. So for the love they showed me I took them shopping, but now I'm broke. Kandy-Cola replied only telling half of the truth.

Casino-Rich looks through the rearview mirror of his car and could see Tatiana, Juicy and Shanelle making trips to the Mercedes Benz, grabbing shopping bags from Gucci, Sachs and Bloomingdales, taking them into the house.

I feel you. You got yourself a real team that ride with you, it's only right you look out for them. I'll wire another $500,000 to your account when we get to the car dealership. I can't have my woman walking around broke that makes me look bad. Casino-Rich replied.

Really Daddy! Thank you. So how good is your concentration? Kandy-cola asked.

Why? Casino-Rich replied with a confused look on his face as he pulls off the block and took a glance at her from the corner of his eyes.

Kandy-Cola licks her lips seductively and leans over towards him and lets her hands travel around his pelvic area and felt his penis growing inch by inch because of her touch. She unbuttons his YSL belt and pulls down his pants as far as they could go along with his boxers. She grabs his hard dick and began jerking it off slowly with a tender touch, then lets her tongue travel around the tip of the head of his dick.

⊓Shhhhh⊓ Shittt! Thank God for tinted windows.⊓Casino-Rich moaned while trying to concentrate on the road while driving.

⊓Mmmm! Mmmm! You taste so good Daddy.⊓Kandy-Cola moaned while working her magic, taking his dick into her mouth deep throating it.

⊓Damn baby.⊓He groaned as he stops at a red light almost running it.

Kandy-Cola twists and turns her head as her mouth went up and down on his dick. Saliva from her mouth drips down his dick onto his balls and she used it as lubrication, jerking him off even faster and harder while sucking on his dick like there was no tomorrow.

⊓You like that Daddy?⊓ She moaned.

⊓Shhhh⊓ Shittt! Hell yea baby, I fucking love it.⊓Casino-Rich moaned.

FETISH

"Who's your bitch?" None of those bitches have anything on me, right daddy?" Kandy-Cola said while sucking his dick like a blow pop.

"Ahhhh! Mmmm! No bitch has a thing on you baby, you're my one and only." Casino-Rich moaned as he found himself yearning for a strange reason, for her to stick her finger into his ass, like she did the first time when she gave him oral sex.

As if Kandy-Cola could read his mind she forces her right hand in between his thighs. Casino-Rich scoops up as she inserts her index finger into his anal. Casino-Rich sat down on her finger as she wiggles and moves it around inside him at the same time sucking and jerking off his dick.

"Mmmm! Ahhhh! Damn!" He groans in pleasure as he pulls over to the side of the road and climaxed, shooting cum straight into her mouth.

Kandy-Cola licks and sucks it all up sending sweet chills through his body. She sat up straight and pulls down the mirror and cleans her mouth and pulls out her brown Mac lipsticks from her purse and puts some on then she pops her lips.

"Damn I think I love you even more. You're turning me the fuck out baby."Casino-Rich said in shock. "I never had a bitch do me like that."

"I aim to please you daddy, but ummm you need to fix your jeans and let's get to the dealership before they close. Kandy-Cola replied while looking at him seductively.

"Yeah, I got this baby."Casino-Rich said and pulls up his jeans and boxers, then pulls off and still couldn't believe what she had done to him. No woman had ever made him cum so fast and so hard before that it made his body tremble.

Tatiana picks up her phone on the third ring.

"What's good heifer? You still with your sugar daddy Mr. Rich, and did you get your new car?" Tatiana said.

"Yup I got the 2012 china white Porsche Cayenne truck with brown peanut butter seats. It's fully paid for and everything is in my name, I'm balling."Kandy-Cola said while laughing.

"Oh shit my bitch has made a come up. What you doing now? Me and the girls are getting ready to hit the streets for a few quick dates then we're heading to Club Perfections, are you rolling? Tatiana said.

Yeah I'll meet y'all there around 2 am. I had him wire another $50,000 into my bank account. I lied and told him I blew all my money, so drinks are on me. Right now I'm following my baby back to his three story mansion in Port Washington, Long Island. I hate going over there. The place is always filled with his low life Goonz Squad niggas and fucking groupie ass dirty hoes, and wannabe video chicks. Kandy-Cola replied.

Word, sounds like a place I need to be at getting my money up, we all can't be Ms. Kandy-Cola and fuck with bosses. Hahaha! Tatiana said while laughing.

Whatever, I'll holler at you later heifer. Kandy-Cola replied and hung up the phone.

She touches the passenger peanut butter leather soft seat while driving and a huge smile spreads across her face.

'I got an $80,000 car all because I'm a sexy bad bitch that knows how to make a nigga nut. Hahaha!' Kandy-Cola said out loud to herself and starts laughing.

FETISH

She sighs, *'aaahhh',* as she pulls up into the circular driveway to the mansion. Twenty luxury expensive cars were lined up in the driveway.

'Damn, I hate being around these under paid niggas I'm to classy for this shit, but let me put on my best fake smile.' Kandy-Cola said out loud to herself as Casino-Rich walks up to the driver's side door and opens it.

She steps out and straightens out her dress.

"You do know I don't like being around all these men, right? You promised me we'd chill at your Condo in the city from now on, and it will be just the two of us." Kandy-Cola said while pouting, but looking him in the eyes seductively.

"I know babe, but bear with me, I have to take care of some things with my people first. We won't be here long." Casino-Rich replied while taking her into his arms.

She leans in and kisses him deeply and passionately. Their tongues dance inside each other's mouth.

"Mmmm." She moans as she felt her pussy getting moist.

A bright flash made them open their eyes and break their embrace.

"What in the hell was that?"

They turned their heads to see four men outside the gate that surrounds the mansion with cameras in their hands taking pictures.

"That's just Paparazzi, they're somewhere over there taking pictures. You will get use it. Just pay them no mind baby." Casino-Rich replied.

"Oh it's nothing new to me boo. I'm Kandy-Cola I'm used to the spotlight. They just caught me off guard." Kandy-Cola responded.

"You and your cocky ass, excuse me boo." Casino-Rich said as he walks off and she follows him inside the mansion.

Right away her facial expression twisted up in disgust. Weed smoke clouds were thick in the air and women were walking around wearing nothing but bras and panties, and more than twenty Goonz Squad members were mangling around the house. Casino-Rich lead her to a room that was decorated in all red, even the red silk sheets.

ⅼSo what you expect me to do!ⅼKandy-Cola asked with a confused look on her face.

ⅼBabe, just stay in here and wait for me. I know you donⅼt like being around a bunch of men. Iⅼl be right back.ⅼCasino-Rich said and kisses her on the forehead and leaves the room not giving her time protest.

He walks up to the third floor and enters a bedroom where two of his Goonz Squad members was waiting and had two naked Spanish women on the bed smoking a blunt. One had dirty blonde hair and the other jet black.

ⅼYo, Smooth and Vedo, here, this is for that work you put in the other night if you know what I mean.ⅼCasino-Rich said as he pulls out a tightly wrapped stack of hundred dollar bills from each pocket and tosses it to them for the shooting they did at the club.

ⅼThanks Boss-man. Youⅼre leaving so soon?ⅼ Smooth said as Casino-Rich turns around to exit the room. ⅼThese two say theyⅼre very big fans of yours.

FETISH

⌐I love your music and would do anything to have your dick inside me.□ The blonde haired Spanish woman said as she gets on her hands and knees showing off her fat ass.

⌐And I just want to taste you.□The one with dark jet black hair said.

The two women French kiss each other seductively.

'Damn I think Kandy-Cola can wait for me a little longer.' Casino-Rich says to himself, as he pulls out a condom from his back pocket and pulls down his jeans and rolls on the condom to his hard dick, then walks over to the bed where the pretty blonde hair Spanish woman was waiting with her as in the air.

He pushes her face down into the mattress and grabs her waist and slowly works his way inside her stoking her wet pussy giving her long strokes. Next to him Smooth smokes a blunt while the Spanish woman with jet black hair sucks on his dick like it was an ice pop, while Vedo fucks her from the back.

'Schmmp', Kandy-Cola sucks her teeth as she checks the time on her iPhone. *'It's been over a half hour, I'm so ready to get the*

hell out of here. I'll give him ten more minutes then I'm gone. Kandy-Cola doesn't wait on any dick, dick waits for me.' She said out loud to herself then smiles when she heard the door open. She gets up off the large bed and walks toward the door then stops. Her smile quickly turns into a frown and a look of disgust appeared on her face as she sees it wasnt Casino-Rich who had entered the room, but his right hand man, Alonzo, who had a black folder in his hand.

Oh God, what are you doing here? Now I know its really time for me to go.Kandy-Cola said as she rolled her eyes and walks pass him.

Alonzo grabs her by the arm.

Not so fast, we have some things we need to discuss.Alonzo said.

Kandy-Cola looks down at his hand that had her by the arm and gives him a warning with her eyes as she places her hand in her purse.

I done told you to never put your hands on me again. Did you think I was playing when I said Id shoot your foolish ass?She said.

FETISH

The tone in her voice causes Alonzo to release his grip.

"I don't have shit to discuss with a low life thirsty ass nigga like you. You're a waste of air and space and a waste of human skin. You can't afford to smell my pussy yet alone afford a conversation with me. I thought I made that clear to you. Your living off a real boss and your just a worker, now get the fuck out my way!" She shouted and bumps him as she grabs the door knob.

"Oh I think you will want to hear me out, you conceited hoe. I found out everything about you. I had to pay a few people to really dig around into your background and nothing came up. You clean your tracks very well, but it seems you done messed up by pissing someone close to you off and they charged me a pretty penny for the dirt on you." Alonzo said with a huge smile on his face.

His words made Kandy-Cola stop in her tracks and spin around in her Jimmy Choo's, showing off a fake smile.

"Listen you pathetic excuse of a man! Anything you may think you found out about me is all a rumors and fake. There for, there's nothing to find because I'm not a groupie, video chick, low life hoe. I'm the Kim Kardashian of the Hip Hop world. I only fuck with bosses, because my pussy is worth it. So stop wasting my time. Kandy-Cola shouted while pointing her finger into his face.

Alonzo just smirks and pushes the black folder into her chest.

What in the hell is this? She replied with a curious look on her face.

I think you should open it and take a look for yourself. Alonzo replied.

'Schmmp!' There isn't shit in here that's going to change what I just told your slow ass. Kandy-Cola started to curse him out some more then stood frozen as she flips through pictures and paper work.

Her heart races, she felt as if she was going to pass out and that her world as she come to know was now at an end.

I see you don't have that smart ass mouth anymore bitch, now do you? Alonzo shouted with a wicked smile on his face.

How? How did you get all of this? Kandy-Cola asked while standing there in shock with her body trembling.

"Hahaha! I told you already, you pissed someone off. The real question you should be asking is what am I going to do with that information if I don't get what I want?" Alonzo said in a sinister tone.

"So you're going to blackmail me and make me pay you for these."Kandy-Cola asks in shock with her eyes wide open, and couldn't believe this was happening. That her past was coming back to hunt her.

"I'm going to make you pay me in more ways than one. I have copies of all these papers. Now come with me."Alonzo said while grabbing her by the arm and leading her out the room and down a long hallway where they made a left turn and pushes her into a huge bathroom.

He unbuttons his jeans and pulls them down along with his boxers.

"You can't be serious right?" Kandy-Cola asked with a look of disgust mixed with disbelief.

"You can stop all that high society conceited crap right now! I have everything on you and hold the cards. I'm going to fuck your conceited ass every time I want to, and you better act as if you love it, or else you won't be able to show your pretty face any more." Alonzo said meaning every word.

"You're really are serious and you're going to do this to me and in this house at that."Kandy-Cola said in disbelief.

"Oh don't you worry, Casino-Rich won't find us. There are twenty bedrooms and nine full bathrooms in this house, and yes I'm going to do this! Shut your ass up!"Alonzo said as he drops the folder and roughly pushes her up against the wall, making her arch her back.

Kandy-Cola's body trembles and felt violated as his hands travels around her thighs. He then squeezes her ass as he lifts up her dress.

"You nasty freaky bitch, you don't even wear panties. That makes it all so much better for me."He groans into her ear as she felt his hot breath as he forces himself inside her womb from the back.

"Ouch!" She moaned as tears stream down her cheek. At least put on a condom, please put on a condom." She begs with tears in her voice.

He mushes her face against the wall, pinning it there.

"I told you, you're no longer in control, I call the shots now!" Alonzo shouted as he thrusts in and out of her.

"Mmmm, damn your pussy is fucking good. I can now see why you make men go insane." Alonzo moaned as his dick got covered in her sweet juices.

He pushes on her back even more making her ass poke up in the air. He slaps her thick brown butt cheek and watches it jiggle as he holds onto her waist and pounds away furiously.

"Yea you can stop acting as if you were too good for me. Now I got my dick all in this pussy. I told I'd get it."He groans as he pushes his dick all the way inside her.

"Ouch! Agghhh! Please put on a condom!"Kandy-Cola screamed while crying.

Tears seem to flow out the corners of her eyes like a waterfall and her facial expression was twisted up in hurt and despair. Not because of the newfound pain in her vagina, but because she was being violated and felt helpless to do anything about it as he controlled her body.

'Please let him hurry up and cum. Please Lord.' She prayed in her head hoping he would finally climax and she could have him out of her body.

The touch of his boney fingers sent a creepy chill through her spine.

Damn you may be crying, but your pussy is saying yes, yes and getting wetter.

Ugghhaa! Ahhh! Ugghh! Damn bitch! He groaned as he climaxes and his body shakes as he lay on her back while she was still crying hysterically.

Get off of me! Get the hell off of me! She cried.

Shut up! Im just getting started. I told you I give the orders here and youre going to get on your knees and let me feel those luscious lips before Im satisfied, and I better not feel any teeth. Alonzo said as he pulls out her soaking wet pussy.

The sound of the bathroom door being busted open causes both of them to scream in reaction from being startled. Ahhhh! Ahhhh!

Then they see the huge frame of D-Wes at the door with an evil stare. He moves to the side and Casino-Rich steps inside the bathroom with a black 9mm Glock in his hand.

"Wait homie! Wait this isn't what it looks like!"Alonzo said as he tries to quickly pull up his jeans.

Casino-Rich charges him, knocking him to ground with his body weight.

"It's not what it looks like! Nigga you're fucking my woman!" Casino-Rich shouted as he swung over and over, postal beating Alonzo in the head.

Blood squirted all over the bathroom floor.

"Ahhhh! Ahhhh!"Kandy-Cola screamed and hollered.

Casino-Rich jumps up off of Alonzo and pimp slaps Kandy-Cola four times.

"You're going to cheat on me in my own house, and with my right hand man! Bitch I'll kill you!"He shouted then punches her in the ribs and forehead, knocking her back against the wall.

FETISH

Alonzo fumbled around with his jeans trying to pull the small 38 revolver from his pocket, but moved to slow.

Boom! A loud sound echoes through the bathroom as Casino-Rich aims and sent a bullet crashing into Alonzo's knee cap.

Ahhhh! Alonzo hollered in excruciating pain, while sitting up and holding what used to be his left knee cap.

You think I don't know you carry a gun in your left pocket. We been friends for fourteen years, asshole! Casino-Rich shouted while bending down and taking the small 3.8 revolver from Alonzo's pocket.

Ahhhh! Ahhhh! Alonzo screams.

It's me, let me explain!

Shut the fuck up. The only reason you're not dead now is because you were my best friend, but if I ever see your face again I'll kill you. I don't care if we bump into each other in the street by accident. I'll kill you and that goes the same for you hoe. You saw your last dime off of me! Get the fuck out my house, the both of you! D'Wes tosses them out! Casino-Rich shouted.

"Wait! Just wait! It's not what you think, don't do this." Alonzo said as Casino-Rich rips the Goonz Squad chain off his neck then D-Wes scoops up Alonzo and throws him over his shoulder, then grabs Kandy-Cola by the hair.

"Look inside the folder! Look inside the folder!" Alonzo shouted repeatedly.

"Shut the hell up pussy!" Casino-Rich said while walking up to him and then punches him in the face two times.

"Uggghhh!" Alonzo groans in pain.

"You can never say you're a part of the Goonz Squad again!" Casino-Rich shouted as D-Wes carries Alonzo away.

The other Goonz Squad members in the house bust out laughing as D-Wes tosses Alonzo and Kandy-Cola outside. The sky got darker and rain began to fall, soaking both of them. Kandy-Cola wipes her tears away and gets up off the ground.

'Thank God there aren't any Paparazzi around to take pictures of this.' She said out loud to herself as the tears escape the corner of her eyes mixed with the rain.

FETISH

'I hope you're satisfied now, you fucking bastard.' She shouted as she stumbles to her truck and hops in and pulls off.

'At least I got to keep the money in my account and my brand new truck. I made sure everything was in my name.' She thought to herself as the rain slows down.

'Like Jay-Z said, on to the next one.' She says to herself then plays her MP3 player in the truck and puts on a Jay-Z song as her motivation trying to forget everything that just happened.

Alonzo held his knee cap tightly as blood ruses out of it mixed with rain onto the drive way concrete.

'I'll get you for this. No one plays me and gets away with it.' Alonzo said out loud as his pride hurt just as much as the gunshot wound.

He managed to leap to his car and start it up. 'You will pay for this Casino, you and that bitch Kandy, I swear.' He mumbled as he pulls off.

'Here Boss, this is the folder that was in the bathroom.' D'Wes said as he enters the giant master bedroom, to see Casino-Rich sitting on the bed with his back turned towards the room door.

His head was hung low as his dreads covered his face as he smokes a blunt and held a 9mm Glock in the other hand.

"Just drop it on the bed and go." Casino-Rich replied without even looking up.

"Are you okay Boss?" D'Wes asked.

"No, I'm not fucking alright! My best friend and right hand man fucked the only woman I decided to wife in the damn bathroom of my own house. I should've killed them both. Now get the fuck out of my room and leave me alone before I take my anger out on you and shoot you in the leg!" Casino-Rich shouted.

"Okay Boss." D'Wes said putting up his hands and back peddling out of the room and shuts the door.

Casino-Rich took three long pulls from the blunt and lets the weed smoke travel through his system, praying it will ease his mind and heart.

'I can't trust anyone, and I have to stay focused on making this money. That should be

my only concern.' He said out loud to himself then looks beside him at the black folder labeled *'Kandy-Cola's Secret'.*

'I shouldn't even care what her secret is, but I do want her back in my life. No woman I know has ever been so beautiful, smart and sexy, and makes me cum like she does.' He said with the blunt between his lips then puts the 9mm Glock down on the bed and picks up the folder.

The curiosity was killing him as he flips the folder open. At first he couldnt make since of what he was looking at. There was a copy of a birth certificate, pictures, and an invoice to a bill.

'Ahhhh! Ahhhh! Nooo! Fucking nooo! It can't be! It just can't be!' Casino-Rich jumps up and screams.

He throws the pictures and picks up his gun off the bed and throws it into the dresser mirror, shattering the mirror into pieces as he went on a rampage destroying the room while screaming.

Kandy-Cola hops out the shower and made a few phone calls, talking to some of her home girls, while putting on her dark green

Mac eye shadow. She works her way into a dark green sleeveless body suit that showed off her voluptuous perfect figure. She slides her feet in a pair of black Jimmy Choos.

'Now off to find the next baller. One monkey doesn't stop any show. I guess Juicy, Tatiana and Shanelle will meet me at the club later on. I'm I heading there early to ease my mind and link up with my other bitches.' Kandy-Cola thought to herself as she locks the front door of the house and hops into her new Porsche Cayenne and pulls off, heading for Club Rain.

She parks her truck across the street from the club and steps out and could feel all eyes on her. Women who envy and hate her stared as men who were driving by or standing in line to get in the club looked at her as if she was a meal to eat. They watched her plump ass switch from side to side. A cheese smile spread across her face when she sees her two friends Cassie and Julia.

⬜Hey girl!⬜They both say simultaneously as they greet her.

They hug each other and kiss on the cheeks.

"Did I have you heifers waiting long?" Kandy-Cola asked.

"No we just actually got here, and we're ready to get some new sponsors." Cassie stated.

"Well let's do this, ladies." Kandy-Cola replied.

The bouncer at the door already knew who they were and let them skip the line and go in. People who were waiting in line curse under their breath. Kandy-Cola waves and smiles at the people she knew in the club. She was happy the club was dark and that her Mac make-up hid her black eye and bruise on her cheeks.

'Damn I got beat up twice for the day, but fuck it I'm going to enjoy my night.' She said to herself as she quickly pushes the negative thoughts from her mind as she and her girls were led to the V.I.P. area and taken to a private table.

The club was jumping, full of people flossing their best outfits and jewelry. A waiter came to their table with two bottles of Moet Rose and a bucket full of ice with Champagne glasses.

⬜What⬜s up with Tatiana, Shanelle and Juicy? Are they coming?⬜ Julia asked.

⬜Yea, they will be here later on. You know Tatiana has to chase that paper first.⬜ Kandy-Cola replied.

⬜Speaking of money, we heard you⬜re living large now and you⬜re Casino-Rich⬜s wifey.⬜Cassie said over the loud music while looking around the V.I.P. area to see what celebrity was there for her to sink her teeth into.

⬜That⬜s a long story.⬜ Kandy-Cola replied.

Chapter 13

Juicy sat in the back seat of Tatiana's Mercedes Benz. Her stomach felt like as if it was doing cartwheels inside as it bubbles up.

'Damn I just want to go home.'

She thought to herself then looks at Tatiana while she was driving. Her eyes turned to Shanelle who was sitting in the passenger seat. They all were dressed as if they were heading to the club, with short tight fitted dresses on, but Juicy knew that wasn't the case. She pulls out her iPhone from her purse then looks up and spoke for the first time since getting in the car.

"Tatiana, ummm, you haven't been having a creepy feeling like someone has been following us these last two days." Juicy asked.

"Hehehehe!" Tatiana and Shanelle both bust out laughing girlishly.

"No Juicy. I swear your innocent ass be killing me sometimes, and yes we're going to have fans, groupies, thirsty niggas and stalkers. It's all a part of having good pussy and that comes with this game, but the .22-Caliber handgun in my purse will shut all there asses down. So you have nothing to worry about we're only going to do two dates then link up with Kandy-Cola and her home girls at the club.□Tatiana replied while still laughing.

Juicy's facial expression turns into a frown as she starts to text her best friend Marvin.

'I'm so sick and tired of this! My sister just won't understand me, but we're heading to a hotel on the Conduit Highway on the border line of Queens to meet three guys. I have this bad feeling like someone is watching us and following me. I keep seeing some weird videos on YouTube that makes me question things.' Juicy wrote and then presses send and receives a new message instantly.

She opens it and begins to read.

'Juicy, I don't know how many times I keep telling you that you're a grown ass woman. You're nothing like your sister or your friends. Just get a normal job like before and leave them alone.'

□Schmmp!□ Juicy sucks her teeth then sighs and began to text.

'You're my best friend, I didn't ask you to put me down. You're supposed to support me and understand me without judging me. I was just venting and it's your job to listen. I will try to get another job, but we're in a recession, work is hard to find, and one day I will break down and explain to you why I can't tell my sister no. She saved my life and it goes back to our childhood. I can't tell you everything through a text or a phone call. I just wanted you to know where I was at while I'm doing these dates for safety reasons.' Juicy wrote and press send and a second later received a new text message. She opens it and began to read.

'Sorry for my attitude, but you know I have your back no matter what Juicy, smh. I have nothing more to say on the subject, because it pisses me off. Anyway, check out this YouTube video. People are saying it's real. There's a maniac going around wearing a sex mask killing people. I think it's true, so watch your back.'

Juicy read then shook her head and clicks on the link at the bottom of the message. The YouTube video loaded and played.

FETISH

"Huh, aaahhh!" Juicy lets out a slight scream and covers her mouth with her hand as she watched a man with his head stuck in the window. You couldn't see his face he was bent over kicking at a man with a leather sex mask on his face, as the man with the leather sex mask bangs in a large piece of broken glass into his anal with a leather paddle that had spikes on it.

The man was hollering in excruciating pain that sounded like an animal being killed.

"Tatiana you have to look at this video on YouTube, it's another one with that maniac with the leather sex mask killing people, it has to be real, and I think this man he killed looks like the same guy we went to see on Sutphin Blvd." Juicy said while pushing the phone up to Tatiana.

Tatiana pulls into the underground hotel parking lot and took the phone out of Juicy's hand.

"Oh shit! Hahaha! Yo, this shit is crazy." She said while laughing.

"It's not funny Tatiana, really pay attention and look closer. That's the same dude's apartment we were in last night." Juicy stated.

"Juicy you're tripping out, you can't even see the guys face, only his ass in the air. I don't know how you figure it's him. Here take your phone." Tatiana said then her heart skips a beat, and beats real slow from what she was hearing on the radio. She turns up the volume.

"But, Tatiana!" Juicy said.

"Shhhh, be quiet Juicy and listen to this." Tatiana said while fanning her hand. "Shanelle go look on Facebook right now!" Tatiana ordered.

Shanelle pulls out her phone from her purse and checks her Facebook news feed.

"It's all over Facebook everybody's talking about it." Shanelle replied with panic in her voice.

"Damn this is really bad!" Tatiana shouted and pulls out her phone.

Kandy-Cola was talking with a new up and coming out music producer. He was covered in jewelry. Right away she could tell that his chain was worth over $100,000. He sat in between her and Cassie trying to spit his best game. The club was packed, music was blasting and people were drinking and dancing, while the gold diggers plotted on their next victims. Kandy-cola looks down at her phone vibrating and lighting up bright on the table next to the bucket of ice. She sees that it was Tatiana's face on the Caller I.D. and picks up the phone.

Bitch where are you? I'm waiting in the club for y'all heifers. Cassie and Julia are with me. Kandy-Cola shouted over the music then puts her finger in her left ear to block out the loud music.

Kandy, baby you need to get the hell out that club now and go home, everybody knows your secret. Tatiana replied.

Huh, what are you talking about Tatiana and how? Kandy-Cola said as she got up off the couch and walks over to a dark corner in the V.I.P. area so she could better hear Tatiana.

It's all on the radio and every social network site, just listen. Tatiana said as she turns up the volume to the radio in her car and puts the phone closer to the speakers as the D.J spoke.

FETISH

"Okay people we're back and live, so if you have been hiding up under a rock for the last five years it will be the only way you never heard of the famous Kandy-Cola. She's a vixen and is known for hosting parties for the most popular clubs, and is really famous for dating entertainers, rappers and singers. Pretty much she's the Kim Kardashian of the Hip Hop world. Her latest meal ticket is Casino-Rich who had climbed the charts with his hits and close to being worth 40 million dollars. I'm here with Roger Towens, who was Kandy-Cola's first man and sponsor, and says the famous Kandy-Cola was born a man and has the pictures and paper work to prove it. The first to leak this story was Alonzo, who is part of the Goonz Squad and Casino-Rich's right hand man, and it's sad to say people, but it's all true. I'm looking at a copy of a birth certificate as I speak." The D.J. said. "So Roger, the floor is yours. Tell the people that's listening what's going on and the story behind Kandy-Cola." The D.J. said.

"Kandy-Cola isn't who everybody thinks she is her real name is Kendal Clark. She's a transgender or transsexual. I'm a hard-working man for the M.T.A. and fell in love with Kendal. I took money from my pension to pay for her sex change, but that wasn't enough for him, he wanted more so I dug into my retirement funds, and damn for a full face and body make over along with plastic surgery. I'm talking about hair implants, butt implants and breast implants. His whole body, making his waist slim, but making his hips and thighs pop out, all to make him look like a Barbie doll. It cost me well over $80,000 and he also had his Adams apple shaved down! Roger shouted.

Wow! You did all of that? You must have been in love with her, I mean him. I'm looking at a copy of the plastic surgery receipt for a Kendal Clark as we speak people and it's all true. Pictures of the receipt and birth certificate are flooding all around Facebook and other social network sites, the before picture of Kendal before his surgery and the picture after the surgery. You can see the resemblance. Okay now, back to you Roger. So does this make you gay? And does this make all the men who slept with her gay? I mean him. And why are you spilling the beans, coming clean and telling after all these years of keeping the secret? The D.J. asks.

Yes I am gay and Kendal was my first and only homosexual relationship. I was in love with him even after he changed his name to

Kandy-Cola and became a woman and yes it makes all those entertainers out there who slept with her gay, because she still don't get off and cum unless she's having anal sex. So no matter what, or how you look at it, at the end of the day you rappers and singers have just fucked a man in his ass without knowing it!"Roger shouted with envy in his voice.

"Ohhh wowww! Hahaha! I love my show right now. The phone lines are blowing up, but back to the main question. Why are you telling now?"The D.J. said in excitement.

Roger sighs before speaking.

"Because, I invested all my retirement money into her body, then took a loan out for a new Range Rover, every year I get a new one for her. I maxed out my credit cards for shopping sprees just to be treated like shit or old news, as if I was no longer good enough for her or worth her time now that rappers and entertainers were her new sponsors. But y'all motherfuckers didn't know the truth, did you? You've all been sleeping with a man. I helped make her, now I'll break her!" Roger shouted with the veins in his forehead throbbing and tears running down his face.

Damn it sounds like someone was whipped and hurt. Hahaha! The D.J. said while laughing. I really wish I could get Alonzo to call into the show to find out the reason behind him being the first to leak the pictures and paper work on twitter. I guess all things aren't good with in the Goonz Squad camp and I wonder if Miss Kandy-Cola is the cause of that. What will this do to the sales of gangster rapper Casino-Rich street credit? Hahaha! Is he now a homo thug on the low or did he already know Kandy-Cola aka Kendal's secret and just went with it. I myself can understand why many men got caught up in her beauty and her fat ass that's on some Nicki Minaj shit. No homo! Hahaha! The D.J. said while laughing.

Kandy-Cola listens and felt as if she was going to pass out. Her heart beats fast in her chest. Sweat drips profusely down her face from nervousness. Tatiana pulled her phone away from the car speaker and puts it to her ear.

Bitch get out that club now and head home, you done messed with too many thugs baby, and I know more than a few of them isn't going take the news lightly and be pissed off. Tatiana said.

FETISH

"Damn it, that fucking Roger, we're going to beat his ass worse than we did this morning. I'm leaving the club now and will see y'all at the house." Kandy-Cola replied and hung up the phone.

She walks back over to her V.I.P. table, to see the music producer that she was talking to a few seconds ago looking at his cellphone then looks at her as if he wanted to punch her in the face as he gets up and bumps her while walking past her.

"I have to get out of here you two can stay if you want." Kandy-Cola said to her two friends Cassie and Julia.

"No girl we're leaving with you. We know everything and by now so does most of the club, every detail and pictures are posted on Facebook and Twitter. People are talking and going in hard on you." Cassie said while getting up with Julia as they grab there things and follow Kandy-Cola as she made her way through the crowd of dancing people.

She could feel all eyes on her, normally she was used to that, but this time it was as if people were envying her or hating on her beauty, but more as if they wanted to attack her and cause her harm.

263

"That bitch is really a transsexual and got a damn man!"She heard someone shout over the music in the crowd of people and people were pointing at her while talking then looks at their cellphones.

"Just keep moving Kandy and fuck what they think or say."Cassie said who was right by her side.

"Kendal you're a dirty ass nigga!" Someone shouted and throws a bear bottle.

She dodges it and it hits someone else.

"You lying, dirty fucking nigga!" More people in the crowd shouted and a few of them spit at her.

She wipes the spit off the side of her face and did everything to keep her composure.

'I can't fight everybody in the club, I just got to get out of here and all I want to do is climb into a dark hole and hide.' Kandy-Cola thought to herself.

"Keep moving we're almost out of here."

"Ouch, you jerk! Whoever just hit me with that, I swear I'm going to fuck them up"

Cassie screams in pain as a bear bottle hit her in the center of her back.

Another one came flying towards her she dodged it and it busts open on the back of Kandy-Cola's head knocking her forward.

"Agghhh!" She screamed in pain.

"Girl you okay?" Julia asks while holding her up.

"Yea I'm okay, I just feel a little dizzy." Kandy-Cola replied and touches the back of her head and felt a wet spot.

She parted her weave with her fingers and felt a deep cut then looks at her hand to see it covered in thick red blood.

"We got to get to the hospital girl." Cassie said.

"Yea you deserve more pain than that bitch!" Someone in the crowd shouted.

Kandy-Cola walks swiftly with her friends. She took a deep breath of relief when she smells the fresh air as she made it out.

"We're taking my truck, I parked across the street." Kandy-Cola said while still feeling dizzy.

"That's fine, but I'm driving you to the hospital." Cassie stated.

It was only midnight and people were just coming out for the night to party. There was a crowd of people trying to get into the club, others standing around just showing off their best outfit. Guys in expensive cars trying to grab up any one they can for the night. Kandy-Cola spotted someone strange moving through the crowd of people on the sidewalk. He stood out right away unlike everybody else who was dressed in their best. He had on an all-black hoodie and looked more like a stick up kid. The man dressed in all black pulls down the hoodie more to cover his face completely. Everything in Kandy-Cola's body told her to run, but she stood frozen as the man in the hoodie approaches her and pulls out a gun.

"Kendal!" He shouted as he stares into her eyes and squeezes the trigger. The first bullet enters her cheek, shattering the bones in her face.

"Boom! Boom!" The gun roars as a bullet slams into her right breast then into her stomach, lifting her up into the air knocking her to the ground.

ᴀAhhhh! Ahhhh! Ahhhh!ᴀ People in the crowd scream and took off running.

The shooter uses them for cover and ran beside them.

ᴀAhhhh! Kandy! Hold on!ᴀ Cassie screams as she bends down to the ground and held her hand.

ᴀSomebody call an Ambulance now!ᴀ She shouted with tears streaming down her face.

Julia pulls out her cellphone and dials 911 while looking down at Cassie and Kandy-Cola who was going into convulsions. Her body was shaking as she coughs up thick red blood that runs out from the corner of her mouth.

ᴀWho did this to you, who?ᴀCassie asks while crying.

Kandy-Cola tries to talk, but only a gasping sound mixed with blood escapes her mouth. Cassie puts her ear closer to her lips as Kandy-Cola mumbles a name in a whisper. Cassieᴀs facial expression tightens up from the name she heard as the Ambulance pulls up and the E.M.T. workers load Kandy-Cola into the back of the Ambulance. Cassie walks off in the opposite direction.

"We're not going to the Hospital to see if she's going to make it." Julia said while crying.

"No, we have something to take care of!" Cassie replied with hate in her voice.

Chapter 14

Juicy knew she was right. The man in the YouTube video they just had watched with the man getting murdered was the same guy that they went on a date with the other night. She felt it in her body.

'So that means the masked maniac man is following us, is that the reason I keep feeling as if someone is watching me. This shit got me stressed out and then Roger's on the radio telling all of Kandy's business. Tonight isn't a good night bad things come in three's, what's next? I should be home.' She thought to herself as they enter the low budget hotel.

They walked pass the Mexican clerk at the front desk in the small lobby. Tatiana leads the way to room 121. She knocks on the door. A light skin complexion tall man no older than twenty-six opens the door. He had on a blue N.Y. fitted cap and was handsome in the face.

⬚Hello ladies.⬚He said.

When he spoke you could see the platinum diamond set of bottom teeth in his mouth.

"Damn this nigga is fine." Tatiana mumbled only loud enough for Juicy and Shanelle to hear.

"Hell yea he is." Juicy replied.

"I'm A and that is my brother Keith." A said while pointing to a light skinned younger version of him with a black fitted cap on.

"And that's my homie Quentin." A said while pointing to a chubby brown skinned man with a red new york fitted cap on with a plastic cup filled with Hennessy in his hand.

"Would you ladies like a drink?" Keith said speaking for the first time showing off his top and bottom platinum diamond teeth.

"Yea that would be nice, but I have to remind y'all time is money so it's how you want to play this out, but you have to pay upfront and extra for any hour we're still here." Tatiana said with her hands out getting straight to business.

A smiled, showing off the diamonds on his bottom teeth.

"Cool, you did say it was $200 apiece for an hour right?" He asks as he digs in his front jeans pocket.

"Yep, and that's a discount, because you're cute." Tatiana replied.

"A" pulls out $600 from a stack of money and places it in the palm of Tatiana's hand. Her eyes never left the knot of money in his left hand that went into his pocket.

"Now that business has been taken care of, I'm ready for that drink." Tatiana said.

"Good because the Jacuzzi is ready." "A" said.

Tatiana turns her head to the side and looks at the large Jacuzzi in the room and began to remove her clothes. Shanelle follows her lead. The three men stared at their beautiful bodies and become aroused as Tatiana and Shanelle ease their way into the hot Jacuzzi filled with bubbles.

"You're not going to get in with them sexy?" "A" asked Juicy while he gets undressed.

"No I'll sit on the bed." Juicy replied. Tatiana and Shanelle was passed cups of Hennessy that they downed straight in one shot and was now working on their second cup.

A gets in the Jacuzzi with only his boxers on. The effect of the Hennessy had taken over Shanelle's body making her horny. Before A could sit down she crawls over to him very seductively. Her slim body was covered in bubbles, but her plump ass stuck out in the air as she made her way towards him with a look of lust in her eyes that said fuck me. She sits up on her knees and rolls up her twenty inch Remy weave into a bun, then grabs his hard dick and pulls it out through the hole in his boxers and stuck it straight into her mouth.

"Mmmm, damn!" He groans as she twists her head from side to side while moaning.

"Fuck, oh damn!" A said through clenched teeth.

Keith got even more aroused from watching their show and gets undressed quickly and climbs into the Jacuzzi. Tatiana leans over to where her purse was on the floor by the Jacuzzi and pulls out a Magnum condom and rips it open then rolls it onto his dick.

"I want you to fuck the shit out of me I'm going to do that dick good." Tatiana said in a slutty tone as she turns around and held the edge of the Jacuzzi with her ass arched up in the air, hanging half way out of the water.

Keith licks his lips greedily and grabs her waist and slowly inserts himself inside her wet warm pussy. He wasted no time thrusting in and out of her with all his might.

︹Yes get in that pussy!︺Tatiana moaned as water and bubbles went splashing everywhere, onto the mirror, walls and on the floor.

Juicy sighs as she turns her head from watching them and was now looking at the male friend they introduced as Quentin. He stares at her with a horny look in his eyes.

'He's cute but too much of a pretty boy. I like the grimy looking thug type or a nerd looking man, a square like my best friend Marvin.' Juicy thought to herself as she takes off her shoes and lifts up her dress then removes her panties.

Quentin pulls out a condom from his jean pocket as he pulls them down and climbs on top of her. He rolls the condom onto his dick and works himself inside her moist pussy. Juicy was pleased and surprised that he knew how to work his dick as he bounce around, hitting different spots in her wet pussy.

⬚Ohhh! Oh shit! Ayyye! Yes!⬚ Juicy moans as she wraps her arms around his neck, squeezing tightly.

He huffs and puffs.

The Stalker taps the tip his finger on the steering wheel.

'I want what is mine and I'm tired of waiting and sneaking around like a cat!' He shouted out loud as he sat in his car in the hotel parking lot in a stolen car.

He grabs the leather sex mask from the back seat and puts it on. Then he grabs the wooden black paddle covered in metal spikes and hops out the car. He walks through the underground parking lot and walks up the stairs and enters the lobby.

The Mexican clerk stares at him.

⬚Hola! ¿Cómo puedo ayudarle?⬚He said in Spanish as he realizes working in the hotel business he had seen it all, as the man with the leather sex mask and a paddle in his hand walks toward him.

There's a woman in the parking lot bleeding, she needs your help. The stalker said in a mumble tone.

Oh Lord! What now! The clerk said as he opens the door that protected him in a small room with bullet proof glass windows from any robberies.

He knew he had made a fatal mistake as the Stalker raises the paddle.

Oh mierda! The Mexican man shouted in Spanish and turns around and tries to run back into the room.

Whack! Whack! That was the only sound you heard as the paddle hits him in the back of his head.

Uggghhh! He groaned in pain as he falls face first into the small office and tries to crawl away and reach for the phone on the desk.

The Stalker grins as he raise the paddle high above his head and comes down with all his strength, cracking open the Mexican clerk's head like a tomato being stepped on by a size fourteen shoes. Some blood oozes out, and a piece of his brain slides across the floor up under the black leather office chair.

The Stalker grabs the master card key and a set of keys to the hotels front door and walks out of the office shutting the door behind him. He locks the glass front hotel doors. He whistles as he walks down the long hotel hallway on the dirty colorful carpet and smiles when he reaches room 1232. He leans his head close to the door pressing his ear against it and could hear loud moaning and groaning sounds coming from different women and men, along with the sound of water splashing. The rage in his body grows. He slides the master card key inside the slot and slowly opens the door and walks in without making a sound.

The first thing he noticed was Juicy on the bed with her legs spread wide open and a chubby brown skin complexion man with his jeans half way down to his ankles, and was thrusting in and out of her.

The Stalker turns his head to see Shanelle giving a tall dark brown skin complexion man with a blue fitted cap on a blow job in the Jacuzzi and Tatiana with her ass up in the as a short guy pounds away.

⎡Ahhhh! Grrrr!⎤ The Stalker screams then growls at the same time.

Everyone in the room stops and froze from what they were doing from the sound and looks at him with a puzzled, confused look on their faces.

⎡Yo homie, you have the wrong room, this isn⎡t that type of S&M party.⎤Keith said as he pulls his dick out of Tatiana and steps one foot out of the Jacuzzi, but before he could get the next leg out he screams in excruciating pain.

⎡Ahhhh!⎤The Stalker swings the paddle, making it crash into his jaw, knocking him backwards.

He falls backwards as he brushes against Tatiana as he fell into the Jacuzzi.

⎡Ayo! What are you doing?⎤ ⎡A⎤shouted as he pulls his dick out of Shanelle⎡s mouth and jumps out the Jacuzzi, then charges at the Stalker while only wearing his boxers.

He took the Stalker down like a pro football player throwing his body weight against the Stalker.

FETISH

"You made a mistake putting your fucking hands on my brother!" A shouts, as he swings a left hook then a right hook punching the Stalker in the face.

"Ahhhh!" Tatiana and Shanelle scream loudly as they watch the fight.

"It's him! It's him! It's the masked man from the YouTube videos!" Juicy screamed repeatedly and pushes Quentin off of her.

Tatiana reaches over the side of the Jacuzzi and starts digging through her purse. The Stalker grunted in pain then spits out blood from his mouth. He smiles when he realizes that A's body was soaking wet from the Jacuzzi water splashing on him when he jumped out so fast. The Stalker digs in his pocket while A continues to send blow after blow to his face. He pulls out the electric Taser from his pocket as A swung a left punch straight into his eye. The Stalker groans in pain as he moves the electric Taser onto the side of A's neck and presses the button.

"Ahhhhhhhh!" A hollered as 400 volts of electricity went through his body causing him to shake and go into convulsions as he falls backwards.

The Stalker stood up off the floor and removes the Taser from ⬛s⬛ neck. Tatiana finally felt the handle to her small .22-Caliber gun in her purse next to her Mac makeup kit and a roll of money. She pulls it out and raises the gun, but she could aim it, her screams echoes throughout the room.

⬛Ahhhh! Ahhhh!⬛

The stalker had placed the electric Taser onto the hand she had the gun in, sending 400 volts of electricity running through her body and traveling through the Jacuzzi⬛s water electrocuting Shanelle and Keith who were now unconscious, floating in the water.

⬛Ahhhh!⬛ Juicy screamed as she panics from seeing her sister and friend in danger and not knowing what to do.

She looks at Quentin who had the same lost scared look on his face as her.

⬛Do something! You⬛re a man.⬛ She said.

⬛So what, that nigga is scary!⬛ Quentin replied.

⬛Ugghh! Gosh!⬛ Juicy said and shook her head and quickly grabs her two high heel shoes off the floor that was next to the bed. She tosses one and it hits the Stalker on the hand with the electric Taser making him drop it next to the Jacuzzi.

Before he could bend down to pick it up Juicy pops off the bed and ran over to him and kicks him in the balls. She screams while swinging her shoe, hitting him in the side of the head.

Ahhhh! Ughhaa! He grunted in pain and fell sideways to the floor face first.

Tatiana! Tatiana! Get up! We have to go! Get up! Juicy said with tears streaming down her cheeks as she did her best to pull her sister out of the Jacuzzi.

Shanelle managed to climb out by herself, breathing hard.

What in the hell happened? Tatiana asked as she opens her eyes.

We don't have time for that. Let's just get the hell out of here! Juicy shouted as Tatiana stood up and grabs her dress and purse off the floor and quickly puts it on and Shanelle did the same.

FETISH

ʺAʺ was regaining consciousness as he groans in pain on the floor and Keith was still knocked out floating in the Jacuzzi while Quentin looks more scared than the women.

ʺCome on letʹs go!ʺ Juicy shouted as Shanelle and Tatiana steps over the Stalkerʹs body with her and opens the room door.

ʺAhhhh! Ahhhh!ʺ Juicy hollered as she felt cold fingers wrap around her ankle.

The Stalker held on tight to her and stares deep into her eyes.

ʺJuicy!ʺ He said in an evil voice that sent chills through her body.

ʺAhahahah!ʺ Juicy screamed while trying to shake her leg free.

Tatiana and Shanelle pull her arms. Quentin, who still hadnʹt gotten up off the bed, pulls up his jeans and hops off, then he runs toward them. He pulls his leg back and kicks the Stalker in the face, like a football player kicking a field goal.

ʺUgghhaa!ʺ The Stalker grunted in pain and releases his grip from Juicyʹs leg, causing her to fall forward into the hotel hallway, knocking Tatiana and Shanelle down and falling on top of them.

Quentin jumps over the Stalker's body and out of the room shutting the door behind him.

"Who in the fuck is that?" He asked out of breath as Tatiana, Shanelle and Juicy quickly wipes their tears and gets up off the floor and walks swiftly down the hotel hallway.

Rage consumes the Stalker as he gets up off the floor then spotted Tatiana's gun that slid up under the bed. He walks over and picks it up.

"Ugghhh!" The sound of A still moaning caught his attention.

"I almost forgot about you." The Stalker said and smiles as he struggles to lift A's body up and places him back into the Jacuzzi next to his brother's floating unconscious body.

"Fuck you! When I see you again I swear I'm going to kill you!" A spit out in a weak voice.

"Not if I kill you first." The Stalker replied with a huge grin on his face as he picks up the electric Taser and stuck it into the Jacuzzi water and presses the button.

"Ahhhhhhhh!" "A" and his brother, scream as the 400 volts of electricity travel through the water, then travels through their bodies.

The water boils up, cooking and peeling their skin off their bodies.

"Ahhh! Ugghhaa!" "A" let out a piercing scream then stops moving.

The Stalker grins as he looks at their burnt skin that turns crispy black and was sliding off their bones like a well-cooked bake chicken.

Tatiana, Shanelle and Juicy along with Quentin ran to the hotel lobby's front door. Tatiana tried to pull it open.

"Hurry up and open the damn door!" Shanelle yelled.

"I'm trying, I'm fucking trying! What do you think I'm doing, pulling on it for my health? It's locked!" Tatiana replied as sweat drips down her forehead.

⬛It can⬛t be locked! Where is the Mexican clerk at?⬛Shanelle said then they all walked to the bubble office surrounded with bullet proof glass.

⬛Ahhhh! Ahhhh! Ahhhh!⬛ They all screamed as they look through the window and see the clerks head smashed open and his brains on the floor in a puddle of blood.

⬛Ahhhh! This shit just can⬛t be happening. Things like this don⬛t happen in real life!⬛ Tatiana screams as tears stream down her checks.

⬛Ahhhh!⬛ Juicy screams as she turns around and could see the Stalker walking towards them whistling with the leather sex mask on his face dressed in all black with the paddle that was cover in spikes with dried up blood on it, in one hand and in his right hand he held Tatiana⬛s gun.

⬛He⬛s coming!⬛ Juicy screamed while crying. I told you we should⬛ve stayed home tonight!⬛

⬛Juicy shut the fuck up and let⬛s go!⬛ Tatiana said as they all look back and could see the Stalker closing in on them.

They took off running to a staircase on the left side of the hallway. They ran up the stairs to the second floor of the Hotel.

Help! Help! Help us! Tatiana, Juicy and Shanelle screamed while banging on room doors as they pass them.

What the fuck! I'm trying to get a nut I paid good money for this room! A dark skin complexion man said as he opens his room door and looks down the hallway to see Juicy, Shanelle and Tatiana and a chubby man running.

The Staler ran up the stairs and sees the man standing halfway out his room door wearing nothing but his boxers. The Stalker raises his right hand with the .22-Caliber handgun in it. The man turns his head and looks at him.

My time isn't up, what the hell going on? I paid Before he could finish his sentence a hole opens up in the center of his head.

He was dead before his body drops to the ground. The woman in his room that lay naked on the bed used the sheet to cover her body and screams in horror as the Stalker steps over her dead lover's body. He ran swiftly over to her and stuffs the small gun into his pocket.

"Ahhhh!" The woman screams and covers her face with the white sheets.

"Please go away! Leave me alone! Go away, God make him go away." She prayed out loud hoping God will hear her cries and the weirdo with the sex mask will go away, but her prayers weren't loud enough. She felt the first blow from the paddle on her stomach.

"Ugghhh! Ahhhh!" She hollered in pain while kicking at him through the sheets.

"Ahhhh! Ahhhh!" She screamed in excruciating pain as the bone in her leg cracks and could be heard breaking into two throughout the room.

"Noooo! Please stop! Help me! Somebody help me! God noooo!" Those were the last screams she made, as the paddle broke her fingers and the arm she used to cover her face.

The bone in her left forearm cracks then brakes through her skin. The bone enters through her mouth as she was screaming. The

Stalker repeatedly swung the paddle over and over.

Ugghhh! Uggaa! Uggaa! She made a gagging sound as her forearm bone went deeper and deeper into her mouth, until it pierced the back of her throat coming out the back of her head, killing her instantly.

The Stalker continues to swing the paddle like a mad man while whistling until the white sheet she was using to cover her body and face was soaked in blood. Red thick blood drips onto the room carpet.

Ahhhh! Ahhhh! Juicy, Tatiana and Shanelle scream as they knock on every room door, but no one opens their door after hearing all the screaming.

One man decides to open his door to see what all the commotion was about and sees the Stalker running towards him with a gun in one hand and a paddle in the next. Oh hell no! He said and quickly shuts his room door.

The Stalker ran around the corner of the hallway and could see Juicy and Shanelle along with Quentin a few feet away. He raises and aims the .22-Caliber handgun and squeezes the trigger three times.

Ahahahah! Juicy screamed as she heard the gun shots and ducks low.

Two bullets enter through Quentin's back and bounce around hitting his organs until one gets stuck in his liver and the other in his heart. He reaches out to Juicy with his hand stretched out, while holding his chest with his right hand with his eyes wide open as he drops to the ground on the hotel's hallway cheap carpet, and dies.

Ahhhh! Ahhhh! He's coming! He's coming! Tatiana screams.

Leave us alone! Leave us alone! Juicy shouted with tears streaming down her face.

I got it! Shanelle shouted as one of the room doors managed to open, that they were pounding on.

They all ran into the room, stumbling over each other as the Stalker calmly walks toward them.

Shut the fucking door! Shanelle yelled. Tatiana slams the door shut and starts pushing the bed in the room towards the door.

FETISH

"Help me!" She said while looking at Shanelle and Juicy.

They join her and push the bed to the door then the round table in the room, along with the nightstand.

"Why is he chasing us? Who is he?" Tatiana said while crying hysterically.

"I told you he's the same guy in the YouTube videos. He's been stalking us for a while now and killing all your dates. What are we going to do?" Juicy said with tears in her voice.

"Hey look, over here." Shanelle said while opening the window on the far side of the room.

Juicy and Tatiana quickly ran over to her and looks out the window.

"We can jump down and run for the car." Shanelle said.

"Hell no we might sprain or break our legs on impact, landing on that hard ass concrete." Tatiana replied.

"Well we don't have that many options. I'd rather have a broken leg or ankle than be dead. I don't about you bitches, but I'm jumping." Shanelle responded then heard a beeping sound that made them all turn around.

The light on the door turns green, letting them know someone was using a card key.

"That nigga got a master key, that's how he got in our room the first time. I'm jumping!" Shanelle yelled then climbs out of the open window and jumps.

"Oouchhh!"She screams as she landed on the hard concrete ground.

Shanelle are you okay?" Juicy asks while looking down out of the window.

"No I hurt my leg really bad and don't think I can get up." Shanelle replied while rubbing her ankle.

"Boom!"Boom!"The sound of the door being kicked startled Juicy and Tatiana.

"Juicy I'm not jumping down there hurting myself then I really won't be able to get away."Tatiana said in a terrified tone as her heart race.

"Okay I got a better idea." Juicy said with her head stuck out the window.

"This is what we will do, there's a window to the next room that's open. So we climb out this window onto the ledge and hold the wall and climb through the other room window. I saw some stairs that lead to the underground parking lot where we should have run to in the first place if we hadn't panicked." Juicy said.

"Okay I'm with it. Get to moving because that bed and table won't keep him out this room much longer." Tatiana said as she looks behind herself and sees the door inching open more and more with each kick the Stalker made, moving the things they used to barricade the door with.

"Shanelle, heifer I don't know how you're going to do it, crawl or hop, but get your ass to the parking lot and to the car. We'll meet you there!" Tatiana said loud enough that only the three of them could hear.

Shanelle shook her head up and down in agreement and wipes her tears.

"Go Juicy, go!" Tatiana screams as she could now she the Stalker's gloved hand in between the room door. "Juicy hurry up and climb out the window, now!" Tatiana yelled.

Juicy climbs out the window and held the wall she could feel the ruff concrete ledge bruise her bare feet as she slowly inches closer and closer to the next room window. Tatiana looks outside the window and could see Shanelle finally standing up weakly and hopping on one leg toward the parking lot.

[Ahhhh! Ahhhh! Tatiana screams as she looks behind herself and could see the Stalker's head squeeze through the room door and almost his whole body.

She climbs out the window not even waiting for Juicy to make it fully to the next window. Her heart was pounding feeling as if it was going to break free through her chest.

[God I just want to go home. Tatiana said as she inches across the ledge closer to her sister and happy that Juicy finally made it to the next room window.

Juicy looks in to the room and could tell no one was inside. The room was completely pitched black. Tatiana stops moving closer to her sister as a weird feeling crept inside her.

[Do you hear that?

[Hear what? Juicy replied.

"That's the point I don't hear anything anymore, the banging just stopped. That can't be a good thing. Move Juicy!"Tatiana shouted in horror as panic consumes her body.

"Okay."Juicy said as she lifts open the room window some more.

"Ahahahahahhhh!" Juicy screams as she felt a glove hand wrap around her leg from inside the dark room.

"Juicy!" The Stalker said in a creepy voice that sent even more chills and fear through her body.

Tatiana inches closer to help her sister but lost her balance and slips.

"Ahhhh!"Tatiana screams as she fell to the ground.

The impact hurt her butt but it wasn't as bad as she thought it would be.

"Ahhhh!" Let go! Let go of me!" Juicy hollered as she could feel the Stalker pulling her into the dark room.

He had managed to pull half of her body through the window.

FETISH

Let go!

Noooo! Juicy screamed and kicks him as hard as she could in the mouth, with the soul of her foot, making him lose his grip and fall backwards.

Ugghhaa! He grunted in pain as he touches his mouth and looks at his glove and sees blood.

Juicy quickly climbs back outside of the window and starts inching towards the room she just came out of.

No Juicy dont go back into the room! Just jump! Jump its not that bad! Tatiana shouted while looking up.

I cant, Im scared! Juicy shouted back while crying.

The Stalker regains his composure and pops up off the floor and screams, Ahhhh! that sound like an animal growling as he runs toward the window.

He stretches his arm out to grab Juicy, but she was out of his reach.

⬚Juicyyyy!⬚ He said in a voice that sounded more like a hissing sound then begins to climb out the window.

⬚Ahhhh!⬚Juicy screams.

⬚Jump Juicy now!⬚Tatiana shouted as she feared for her sister⬚s life.

Juicy held her breath and jumps backwards off the ledge of the window and landed on her feet but falls to her butt.

⬚See I told you, it wasn⬚t that bad. Let⬚s get the hell out of here!⬚Tatiana said as she helps Juicy off the ground.

Tatiana and Juicy both look up to see the Stalker staring down at them from the window. His eyes were cold and dead and in the blink of an eye he just disappeared.

⬚Run!⬚ Tatiana shouted knowing after seeing to many movies that it wasn⬚t a good thing when the killer disappears like that.

They ran to the underground parking lot.

⬚I see the car over there.⬚ Juicy said while running and pointing to the Mercedes Benz s430.

Tatiana jumps in the driver seat and pulls her keys out her purse and starts up the car. Juicy hops into the passenger's seat and locks all the doors as her heart race and her stomach bubbles up in fear.

"Where's Shanelle. I told that heifer to meet us by the car."Tatiana said while wiping her tears away.

"Do you think he got her?" Juicy said with her facial expression balled up in sadness.

"No bitches I'm back here, can we get the hell out of here now?"Shanelle said after popping up off the floor of the back of the car.

"What are you doing on the car floor?" Tatiana asked puzzled.

"Bitch I'm not stupid. There's an insane killer running around and my dumb ass wasn't going sit up straight so it would make it easy for him to find me! I don't think so! Now can we please get out of here?"Shanelle shouted.

Tatiana steps on the gas and pulls off. Just as she was about to exit the underground parking lot she stops.

Why in the hell did you stop? Shanelle asks then looks at Juicy and Tatiana who was trembling in fear.

Shanelle looks ahead to see what they were staring at and her eyes open up wide as a quarter of a tear slowly run down her cheek. The Stalker was standing in front of the underground parking lot exit staring at them through his leather sex mask. In one hand was the black wooden paddle that had spikes on it, dripping fresh blood onto the ground, and in the next hand he grips Tatiana's chrome .22-Caliber handgun.

Run his ass over Tatiana! Shanelle shouted.

I'm already ahead of you. Tatiana replied as she pops the car gear into neutral and rams the gas.

I'm going to kill this sick twisted asshole! Tatiana said through clenched teeth as she shifts the gear into drive.

The rear tires spin burning tire rubber as it took off.

Die fucker! Tatiana shouted and to her surprise the Stalker dares not to move.

He licks his dry lips in a sick twisted way then stuck the gun inside pocket and took off running toward the car as it came at him head on. He jumps and ran on to the hood of the car, then the roof.

"Oh shit this nigga thinks he's a Ninja. Did he just jump over the car?"Tatiana said as she pulls out the parking lot at full speed and onto the highway.

"No he's on top of the car!"Juicy yelled as she seen a part of his hands by her window.

The Stalker held onto the car as he lay flat on the roof. He swung the paddle trying to break the driver side window.

"What the fuck!"This guy just won't give up!"Tatiana shouted.

"Shake him off the car Tatiana!" Juicy shouted.

Tatiana steps on the gas speeding down the North Conduit Highway. She swerves the car from left to right, but the Stalker held on.

"Beep!" "Beep!"Other cars beep there horns from seeing the crazy driving Tatiana was doing.

⌈Everybody hold on!⌉ Tatiana said and did a sudden hard full stop, stomping on the breaks.

The Stalker flew forward off the roof of the car and onto the concrete floor.

Juicy, Tatiana and Shanelle look on in horror as he lay still in the middle of the highway then starts to move.

⌈Run him over!⌉Shanelle screamed.

Tatiana steps on the gas and the car pulls off. The Stalker rolls just before the Mercedes Benz crashes into his head then he pops up and dodges a speeding car on the highway. Tatiana looks in her rearview mirror while Juicy and Shanelle turn their head around looking behind them. They all could see the Stalker clearly standing in the middle of the highway with the paddle in one hand as he raise his left hand high and stuck out his middle finger as their car sped away.

Chapter 15

Casino-Rich ran as fast as he could for three blocks and turns the corner, running up another block with the smoking gun still in his hand. He hops into his BMW 6 series coupe and pulls off while tucking the 9mm luger under the passenger seat while stopping at a red light. He removes the black hoodie to reveal a tan Gucci shirt with his green bird squad medallion chain hanging from his neck.

'That nigga thought he could play me and have the world thinking I'm gay and nothing would happen. Hell fucking no! Fuck you Kandy-Cola or Kendal, whatever your name is. I got something for Alonzo's ass as well, when I catch up to him.' Casino-Rich said out loud to his self as he pulls up behind a club on the next side of Manhattan, far from where he just had shot Kandy-Cola in the face and chest.

He held his head down as flashes of the pictures of how Kandy-Cola really looked before her plastic surgery. Then he thinks about the copy of the birth certificate and invoice of payment for the bill of her sex change that was all in the folder Alonzo had left in the bathroom. The same information he wished he'd only had access to, but was now all over every social network site in the world and so was the interview with Roger on the radio.

Casino-Rich steps out his car and kept his head low as he made his way through a back alleyway to the back of the club. A fat heavy set bouncer opens the back door as he approaches. Casino-Rich digs in his pocket and passed him a knot of money that came up to ten thousand dollars.

'Remember this never happened or you won't live long enough to spend that money.' Casino-Rich stated.

The bouncer shook his head up and down with fear in his eyes as Casino-Rich enters the club and the bouncer shuts the door behind him.

'I got the perfect alibi for when the police are looking for a suspect for Kandy-Cola's murder. I can't be blamed. Everybody has seen me in this club all night and I was only gone long enough to use the bathroom.' Casino-Rich thought to himself and walks to the bathroom where his bodyguard D'Wes was waiting with

his arms folded, guarding the door as if he was in it.

Come on let's go! Casino-Rich ordered.

D'Wes uses his massive body to lead the way through the club filled of partying people. Casino-Rich did his best to hold his head high but could feel eyes on him while people look at their cellphones. He knew that they were questioning his manhood and wondering if he was gay or not, a homo thug on the low. D'Wes leads him to the V.I.P. area where they had a seat waiting. Casino-Rich wasted no time to grab a bottle of Ciroc and drank straight from the bottle hoping it would help drown his pain and the feeling of his pride being hurt. He could see two of the Notorious Gang members Red-Banger and Blue-Banger with a few of their people drinking and having fun in the V.I.P. area. He scans the area some more and see a few entertainers with their team, ten or sixteen people deep. Casino-Rich busts out laughing like a crazy man.

Do you believe this shit, D'Wes? All the shit I did for every one of the Goonz Squad members. I brought them cars and homes, even women and put them on a payroll, just for them all to leave me high and dry when shit hits the fan, as soon as everyone thought I was a homo thug!❑ Casino-Rich shouted while guzzling more Ciroc out the bottle.

❑Yo I❑m still here for you homie, but you know that❑s how people are, they❑re around when you❑re on top and feeding them, but as soon as you hit a problem or a speed bump in the road they❑re gone.❑D❑Wes said.

❑Shut the fuck up. I didn❑t ask for your opinion nigga. You think I❑m gay too, don❑t you!❑ Casino-Rich shouted while reaching for his waist where he kept the 9mm luger he used to shoot Kandy-Cola.

❑No I don❑t, but if you❑re going to act like this, I quit nigga! Now you❑re really on your own you homo thug motherfucker!❑D❑Wes shouted back as he gets up and puts his hand on his waist where his gun rested.

Casino-Rich❑s facial expression tightens up in anger. He looks around and could see people in the club staring at him and D❑Wes.

❑You❑re lucky fool, there❑s too many witnesses right now, but watch your back because I will be coming for that ass.❑Casino-

Rich said and his words were slurred from being drunk.

"Hahaha!" D-Wes laughs.

"Homo thugs always come after ass so whatever nigga, I'll be ready." D-Wes said as he walks away.

'Damn bastard, I don't need any of them, fuck the Goonz Squad, I made them.' Casino-Rich said as he sat back down pulling out a fresh bottle of Ciroc from a bucket of ice, then he felt the weight of the couch shift on both sides of him.

He looks on his right to see a beautiful light skin complexion woman with curly hair with luscious lips and a gorgeous smile with smile.

"You're the famous Casino-Rich? I'm Brandy and that's my friend Kayenne." The woman said. Casino-Rich turned his head and looks at the woman on his left to see a beautiful brown skinned female, with chestnut dreads in her hair.

"Yea that's me!" Casino-Rich said as he looks at both the women with lust in his eyes.

FETISH

The Ciroc was making him hornier than usual.

"Well we're big fans and will do anything to be with you even if it's just for one night. You can fuck us both, however you like." Brandy said while biting her bottom lip seductively.

Casino-Rich head bobs from feeling intoxicated.

"That's what's up let's break out of this place. Can you drive I'm too twisted to drive and I just fired my bodyguard." Casino-Rich says while pulling out his car keys and passing them to Brandy.

"Yes I can drive Daddy."

"Let's go." Casino-Rich said as they get up and make their way out of the club.

Casino-Rich gave Brandy directions to his Condo in Manhattan.

He now sits in his all white bedroom on his King size bed only wearing his boxers with a half empty bottle of Peach Ciroc in his hand taking huge gulps from it, wondering how they got to his Condo so fast. He watched Brandy and Kayenne undress to their panties and bras, kissing each other caressing each other's bodies. Brandy walks over to him seductively and bends down getting on her knees.

'Damn this bitch has a beautiful face.' Casino Rich thought to himself as he stares at her luscious lips and brown eyes and neatly curly hair.

She pulls down his boxers and smiles as she grabs his rock hard, thick dick and took it into her mouth.

Mmmm! Casino-Rich moans as he closes his eyes and the sensation of her wet mouth sent sweet chills through his body.

Images of Kandy-Cola giving him the best head in his life play in his mind.

'Stop it, stop thinking about her. She's not even a real fucking woman.' He said in his mind over and over.

Kayenne walks over to them. She took three red pills out of her bra and grips them tight in the palm of her hand as she bends over and sees that Casino-Rich eyes was shut. She slowly kisses his neck and lets her tongue travel down and around the tattoo on his chest. She checks to make sure that his eyes were still closed. She opens her palm and drops the three red pills into the bottle of Ciroc that was in his right hand. Casino-Rich pops open his eyes as soon as she did. Kayenne's heart raced, she knew the Ciroc bottle was clear and if he looks at it he would see the red pills sitting in the bottle slowly dissolving.

"Mmmm!" He groans in pleasure from Brandy's skills, as her head twists from side to side and she works her magic putting spit all over his dick while jerking it off and sucking the tip of it.

She removes her hands and deep throats his dick, stuffing it all the way down to base of his dick.

"Mmmm!" She moans as she gasps for air with a thin string of pre-cum connected to her lips from his dick.

She wipes her mouth while sucking her index and middle finger.

"I want you to fuck the shit out of my mouth. Treat me like a slut, like the shit you rap about in your songs baby." Brandy moaned with lust in her eyes.

Casino-Rich grins then took three huge gulps from the bottle of Ciroc and swallowed the pills without knowing it. Kayenne and Brandy smile devilishly. Casino-Rich noticed Brandy had slowed down her pace so he grabs the back of her head forcing it down. She opens her mouth taking his dick as far as she could as he pump her head up and down, fucking her mouth as if it was pussy. She moans while she slobs down his dick like a Porn Star.

Mmmm! Uggaa! Shit yes! Casino-Rich groans then felt dizzy.

He fell flat onto his back on the bed and the bottle of Ciroc that was in his hand was slowly spilling all over the sheets.

'Damn I drunk way to fucking much, I can barely move and my stomach hurts.' He said with his facial expression balled up in pain and he felt as if he was about to vomit, but didn't have the strength to move.

He couldn't even lift his arms up. He turns his head and looks at Brandy and Kayenne standing next to each other looking like Cover Girl models.

Is everything set up? Brandy asked Kayenne.

FETISH

"Yep, I got my iPhone recording everything. It's sitting on the dresser aiming at the bed and I'll use your phone to take pictures."Kayenne replied.

Casino-Rich heard everything they said, but was powerless to move. He tries to keep his eyes open and watch their movement as a cheese smile weakly spread across his face as he sees them pull down their panties and step out of them. He admires their beautiful shapes and curvy bodies with thick thighs. Then his eyes open wide up in shock as they spread their legs and pull out dicks that were as big and wide as his that they had tucked away, hiding between their legs the whole time.

"What the fuck!"It took all his strength to mumble as he stares at the beautiful woman walk toward him while jerking their dicks making it even harder. Brandy flips him around and forces him onto his hands and knees.

"Wait! Wait! What in the hell is going on here! Ahahahah!" Casino-Rich hollered as Brandy forces her dick inside him while holding his waist.

"You like that right?" Brandy grunted with anger as she thrusts in and out of Casino-Rich's ass.

FETISH

⌐Uggaaaahhh! Ahhh!⌐ He screams weakly, but his scream was cut off as Kayenne forces her eight inches of brown skin dick into Casino-Rich⌐s mouth.

She pulls his long dreads as his head nods off. He tried to bite down on her dick but couldn⌐t control his body and didn⌐t know why and gets angrier at himself as he became aroused and his dick grows hard.

⌐You like that don⌐t you?⌐Kayenne said as she fucks his mouth.

⌐Ahhhh! Arrgghh!⌐ He tries to scream, but almost chokes as Kayenne hits the back of his throat.

⌐Mmmm, yes!⌐Brandy moaned as she pulls out and nuts on his butt cheeks then Kayenne change positions.

Kayenne locks her fingers into his dreads and yanks his head back like a woman.

⌐Just stop, please stop, ahhhh!⌐ He screams as she enters his ass, ripping it open even more.

Her dick was thicker than an Italian sausage the smell of feces was mixed with blood was in the air. Kayenne pulls her dick out her mouth and gets off the bed and gets her purse that was on the phone and pulls out the iPhone and aims it taking pictures.

☐I need some good shots of his face and the Goonz Squad chain. Turn his head towards me.☐Kayenne said and Brandy grabs his neck while holding his head up and turns it towards Kayenne as she took pictures.

After, Brandy rolls Casino-Rich onto his back and sucks his dick until it was nice and hard and wet. Then she eases on top of him and slowly works his dick inside her ass.

Casino-Rich fought back his tears as he felt her dick slapping him on the stomach as she rode him, bouncing up and down. He tenses up as he felt himself about to come. Brandy hops off him and took his dick into her mouth catching all his thick white cum and rubs his dick all over her face and lips then gets up.

☐Did you get all of that?☐She asks.

☐Yep, I got it all girl.☐Kayenne said as she tucks her dick back between her legs and puts on her panties on and works her way back into her dress.

Brandy did the same. They both walk back over to Casino-Rich who was on the bed, lying on his back barely able to move with his dick still hard. He turns his head and looks at them.

"I swear I'm going to kill you niggas when I catch you." Casino-Rich said in a weak voice meaning every word.

"Hahaha!" Brandy and Kayenne laugh as Brandy flips her hair back.

"Hmmm, just like you did to our best friend Kandy-Cola. Yes we know that it was you who shot her earlier tonight. She seen your face and whispered your name before the Ambulance came and took her away. As you may guess my name isn't Brandy and hers isn't Kayenne. I'm Cassie and this is Julia, we don't use our birth names, because it's not who we are anymore. We don't care if you find us and kill us we're just ruining your career and life. We recorded everything that just happened and uploaded it to YouTube. It already has over two hundred thousand viewers and it's still rising. Next we're going to share and post the video on Facebook along with the pictures and on Twitter, then the world can clearly see that Casino-Rich the gangster rapper isn't nothing more than a homo thug that just got fucked by two sexy bad ass transsexuals.□ Cassie said while laughing and she and Julia make their way out of the room smiling while posting pictures on twitter.

They made their way out of the Condo. An hour passes and Casino-Rich was finally able to move again, the effect of the rape date rape drug had finally worn off. He slowly sits up on the bed and could now feel the pain from his anal travelling up through his spine. A tear escapes the corner of his eye as he digs in his jean pocket that was on the floor and pulls out a small touch screen phone and logs into his Twitter account. Anger rose in his body as he watch the video of him that was posted on Twitter and the posts of pictures of him having sex with two transsexuals, looking like he enjoyed it.

'The gangster rapper is no real thug he's just a homo thug.'

'I won't be supporting him and buying any of his music.'

'I wouldn't listen to it if someone gave it to me for free, real talk.'

FETISH

'I bet the whole Goonz Squad takes turns fucking each other.'

Casino-Rich read all the post and knew for a fact his career as he knew it to be was now over.

'Those two transsexuals just fucking killed me without a gun! My life, my respect, everything I worked hard for is done, it's over!' he said to himself while crying.

He picks up his 9mm luger handgun off the floor and placed the barrel of the gun into his mouth and starts to squeeze the trigger.

'Damn I can't go out like that. I just can't kill myself, I just can't.' He said as he pulls the gun out his mouth then he hears a clicking sound of a gun from behind him.

⬚I can!⬚A voice boomed.

Casino-Rich turns around to see Alonzo standing their pointing a chrome .45-handgun at his head. Before Casino-Rich could raise his gun and pull the trigger, Alonzo squeezes the trigger to his chrome .45-handgun twice.

The first bullet rips off the top half of Casino-Rich⬚s face sending it flying to the floor. The second bullet rips into his cheek and jaw and came out the back of his head killing him instantly.

'I told you I'll come back for you.' Alonzo said as he spits on Casino-Rich's dead body as he stares at it all twisted up on the floor, then turns around and walks away

Chapter 16

Tatiana pulls up in front of her house and parks the car. She turns her head to the side and looks at Juicy in the passenger seat making a phone call.

Who are you calling Juicy?

I'm calling Red. She replied.

Who Red-Banger, why? Tatiana asked with a puzzled look on her face.

They all new Red-Banger, he was like a brother to Tatiana and Juicy but on the streets he was a notorious gang member that he demanded respect and fear for. Red-Banger answers the call after the second ring.

What's good Juicy? I read your text, who are you having an issue with? I'll come over now with some soldiers now. Red-Banger said.

Before Juicy could get a word out her mouth Tatiana snatches the phone in the blink of an eye.

Hello Red, it's me Tatiana.

"What's good Sis, what's going on? Juicy got me concerned and you already know I'll lay a nigga down for y'all in a heartbeat." Red-Banger replied.

"I know, but it's not even that type of party love, I know you have your own problems going on. It's all over the streets about the crime family."Tatiana replied.

"Yea that's true, but I'll still look out for y'all we're peoples and go way back." Red-Banger responded.

"Really it's okay. Just one of my dates got out of control, but it was handled."Juicy is just overreacting it was her second time coming on a date with me."Tatiana said.

"Aright, if you say so, she made it seem like it was deeper than that. You know I don't judge what y'all do for a living, because I'm no better, but you have to be careful out here. Anyway, don't ever hesitate to call if you got a problem."Red-Banger stated.

"Cool and I won't, later Red." Tatiana said.

"Later mami." Red-Banger said and hung up the phone.

"Why did you do that for? Red could've helped us." Juicy said and couldn't believe what her sister had done.

"Juicy we can't call Red-Banger for every little crazy nigga we encounter, a nigga like that you use when you really need him. It's like calling in the army, and if you call him for little problems it's like crying wolf and he won't come when we really need him." Tatiana replied.

"And we don't need him? We had a psycho chase us and kill people.

"Okay let's call the police or go to the police station. We have to tell them what happened. Why are we here at the house?" Juicy said as she couldn't believe that they came straight home after barely escaping with their lives from an insane stalker.

"Juicy you know I hate the police! I been to jail once, because I was trying to protect you and I'm never going back again! So fuck them alright! We're home and we're safe, that's what matters!" Tatiana shouted while looking at her sister.

"Well can we at lease take Shanelle to the hospital?" Juicy responded.

"Schmmp!" Tatiana sucks her teeth and turns around and looks at Shanelle in the back seat.

"Do you want to go to the hospital?" Tatiana asks.

"Naw I'm good, the fall from the jump wasn't that bad I just hurt my ankle a little, but its fine now." Shanelle replied.

"Both of you are out your damn minds. You don't find it strange this psycho was only chasing us. You didn't want to let Red-Banger get involved, or call the police, or go to the hospital. I just don't understand you two!" Juicy shouted with a confused look on her face.

"Juicy you need to stop acting like a child. Things like this happen in the real world and come with the business. We just have to deal will it and I got something special in the house just in case anyone pops up unexpected." Tatiana says as she tries to control her anger from getting mad from debating with her sister.

"Why can't you both see that this just isn't right, who the hell is he? I'm scared and that stalker killed a lot of people in that hotel tonight, but mostly he was after us! He even knew my name. I heard him say it when he grabbed my leg!◻ Juicy shouted as tears stream down her cheeks.

◻Juicy clam down he probably heard me say it when we was running.◻Tatiana said.

◻You◻e stupid if you think I believe that shit Tatiana!◻ Juicy shouted while crying and opens the car door and steps out the car slamming the door behind her and walks to the house.

She stops in her tracks when she notices that all the lights in the house were off. She flinched when she heard a noise behind her and relaxes when she sees it was just Shanelle and Tatiana.

◻Why haven◻ your butt unlocked the door yet? I have to pee.◻Shanelle said.

◻Oh her ass is probably scared.◻Tatiana said causing her and Shanelle to laugh as she digs in her purse and pulls out her house keys and unlocks the door.

She walks in and turns on the living room light and rushes to the first floor bathroom.

"You heifer, you know my leg still hurts and I have to pee. Now I have to walk all the way upstairs!"Shanelle shouted as she made her way up the stairs with an attitude.

"You were to slow chick!"Tatiana said while laughing from the bathroom.

Juicy sat down on the couch and folded her arms trying to stop her mind from over thinking and the tears from flowing. She felt her phone vibrating letting her know she had a new text massage. She digs in her purse and looks at the text that was from her best friend Marvin that read

'Are you okay?'

Juicy texts back.

'O.M.G. you have perfect timing. No everything is not okay I'm having a nervous breakdown. Please come over I need a bottle of Moet and seriously talk to you.' She wrote and press send then gets a new text message in a matter of seconds.

'I'll be there in a half hour.'

Juicy smiled when she read the message then turns her head to see Tatiana running out her bedroom holding a long black object.

Tatiana what is that? Juicy asks.

This right here little sister, is a pump shotgun and is the reason you don't have to worry about sleeping good tonight. We're safe in this house and in the morning I'll call one of my tricks and give him a freebie or trade some pussy for some smaller guns. Tatiana said.

Do you even know how to use that thing? You're so small that gun looks bigger than you. Juicy replied.

I know how to use it. What could be so hard, you pump and aim and squeeze the trigger. Tatiana replied.

Whatever, where's Shanelle? Juicy asks.

That skinny bitch is still upstairs stinking up the bathroom, taking a shit. Tatiana said while laughing.

Ummm, where's Kandy-Cola, she was supposed to meet us here over an hour ago? Juicy asks.

FETISH

Damn you're asking a lot of questions, but you're right, between all that happened to us at the Hotel I almost forgot that Roger had told the world she's really a transsexual. Call her phone. Tatiana said.

Juicy scrolls through her phone until she sees Kandy-Cola's picture and name then presses call and puts the phone to her ear.

It's just going straight to her voicemail. Juicy replied with a worried facial expression.

Something's wrong, she always answers her phone for us even if she has a dick in her mouth. Tatiana responded.

Ahhhh! Noooo!

Juicy and Tatiana heard Shanelle scream from the bathroom upstairs then she comes running out the bathroom and down the stairs with her phone in her hand.

Why are you screaming like that crazy homeless woman that be down the block. Tatiana said as she grips the pump shotgun ready for anything and could see the tears streaming down Shanelle's face.

It's all over Facebook and Twitter. Shanelle said with tears in her voice.

FETISH

⬛What⬛s all over Facebook and Twitter, what are you talking about? You⬛re not making any since.⬛ Tatiana replied while putting the shotgun down next to the kitchen entrance way.

Shanelle wipes her tears and took a deep breath.

⬛Someone shot Kandy-Cola two times when she was leaving the club!⬛Shanelle said.

⬛Noooo! Noooo!⬛Juicy and Tatiana both screamed simultaneously and starts crying.

They both pull out there phones and log on to their Facebook accounts while still crying.

⬛Wait it says she⬛s still alive just in critical condition in the I.C.U. at the Bellevue Hospital in Manhattan.⬛Juicy said.

⬛So what are we waiting for? Grab your purses, where out of here!⬛Tatiana said.

Shanelle was the first one to gather her things and to reach the door. All she could think of is was Kandy-Cola dying alone. They didn⬛t always see eye to eye, but they loved each other all the same. Shanelle opens the front door and stops in her tracks and stood frozen. All she seen was a black shirt then she looks up and stared into the cold dead eyes of the Stalker.

Ahhhh! She screams and swung at him, connecting two punches to his face.

The Stalker steps back and swung the paddle up like an upper cut punch, knocking Shanelle in the chin, a cracking sound echoes throughout the house letting him know her jaw was broken as she flew backwards up in the air, but not before she scratches at his eyes and grab the leather sex mask off his face.

Juicy was still by the couch when she seen Shanelle's slim body hit the floor. Tatiana grabs the shotgun against the wall by the kitchen and aims, but froze as her and Juicy's heart race with fear as they stared at the Stalker's face. It looked as all the skin on his face had been ripped off. He had no hair on his head or any eyelids or lips. His face was a dark red, brownish color.

It can't be! Tatiana said as her and Juicy's mind went deep into a trance as they thought the last day they ever seen him played out through their minds.

The two police officers had their guns pointed at ten year old Juicy who was in a headlock and naked. Dustin used her as a shield. Twelve year old Tatiana's smile quickly was wiped away. *'This wasn't part of the plan for them to get him to stop raping us and he uses her as a shield.'* Tatiana thought to herself.

Drop the little girl and put your fucking hands up, you pervert! One of the police officers shouted.

Fuck you! You won't take me alive! I'm not going to jail! I'll snap this little slut's neck first! Dustin spit back as he squeezes tighter choking Juicy even more.

Help me Tatiana. Juicy was barely able to get the words out.

Tatiana's body trembled then she smiles as she remembers the second part of her plan to make sure Dustin would never be able to rape them or any other woman again. She walks passed the police officers whose full attention was only on Dustin and Juicy. She walks by a table in the small kitchen then bends down and goes under the kitchen sink and opens up a cabinet then grabs a large tomatoes can.

Ouchhh! She groaned and was caught off guard and shocked that it was still hot.

Living in the Bronx on 149 and Southern Blvd she had seen a lot on the streets. The other day she was walking to the store and seen a few police officers run up on a well-known neighborhood drug dealer who would always try to talk to her even knowing she was young. She watched him run to a car, lift the hood and drop a pack of his drugs in the car battery. The police officers harassed him but with no drugs they had to leave him alone. Tatiana walks over to him.

Why did you throw your drugs in the battery? She asked curiously.

The hustler looks at her with lust in his eyes as he stares at her young undeveloped body and could tell that she was already sexing.

I put my stash in the battery acid because the acid can eat everything and dissolve it. The hustler replied.

Does it also work on flesh? Tatiana asked.

The Hustler stared at her strangely before answering her.

Yea, I said everything.

Okay can you please pour some in a can for me? Tatiana asks then she runs over to a plastic garbage can that was by her building and quickly returns over to the hustler by the truck.

He continues to stare at her strangely then turns around and pulls the battery out of the truck.

Keep your hands steady. If I spill one drop of this on you it will eat right through to your bones. I'm not even going to ask what you want this for, but you owe me. He said as he pours the battery acid into the can.

Thank you and I'll pay you back. Tatiana said and walks away.

The hustler watches her little ass shake as she walks. The next morning as soon as her mother went to work Tatiana knew she only had an hour before Dustin would wake up and make his way to Juicy and her room. She carefully pours the battery acid into a small black pot and puts it on the stove until it was bubbling, then pours it back into the large tomatoes can and grabs a cloth to hold it and place it up under the sinks cabinet.

She now had the large can in her hand making her way back towards the room. The only one who noticed her was Juicy praying her sister will save her as Dustin⬚s bicep tighten around her neck. Tatiana looks into Juicy eyes and mouths the words 'bite him", while she chops down with her teeth. It took Juicy a few seconds to understand what her sister was saying because of a lack of oxygen, but when she did she opens her mouth wide and bites down as hard as she could onto Dustin⬚s bicep.

⬚Ahhhh! You little bitch!⬚ Dustin screamed in pain, but squeezes tighter and refused to let go of his grip in fear of the Police officers.

Juicy sunk her teeth deeper into his flesh until she could taste his warm blood in her mouth. Dustin couldn⬚t take the pain no more and toss her to the floor. Juicy rolls naked towards the police officers. Tatiana smiled wickedly and steps in close to Dustin and tosses the battery acid onto his face. The hot battery acid ate through his hair on his head and ate through the skin on his face, melting his eye lids and lips off and burnt the skin on his chest and back. He drops to the floor and rolls around. Smoke eases off his body as if he was being cooked alive.

Ahhhhhh! Ahhhhhh! It burns, it burns! Ahhhhhh! He screamed in excruciating pain.

The police officers, Juicy and Tatiana look on in horror as Dustin got on his knees and screams while looking at them. His face was melting off. One of the police officers grab a blanket off the bed and throws it on Dustin doing his best to wipe the acid off as he did so he peals away more of Dustins flesh from his face and the acid burns through the blanket and burns the police officers palms, causing him to jump back in pain and watch Dustin roll around.

Dustin finally stops moving and passes out unconscious from agonizing pain. The police officer handcuffs him.

Damn she really did a number on him. One of them said.

Good he deserved it. The next one said then looks at Tatiana. So what should we do with her? He asks.

"Handcuff her we have to arrest her and take her in, even though she's a victim but what she did was a crime." The other officer replied.

Dustin got eighteen years to life for statutory rape from raping minors. Tatiana had to go to juvenile jail for nine months for assault charges, even though she was a victim. Juicy and Tatiana's mother Heather despise them both ever since that day. She didn't care that Dustin had raped them for years. All she cared about was him and the fact her daughters took him away, the only man that wanted her and another paycheck out the house. She beat them for any mistakes they made using it as an excuse to take out her anger and hate for them.

Tatiana couldn't take the abuse no more and starts prostituting at the age of sixteen with a master plan. At the age of nineteen she had saved enough for a down payment on a house in Far Rockaway and took Juicy with her. Heather was more than happy to see them go as she went into a deep depression, eating and becoming overweight cursing the day she pushed out her children.

Juicy and Tatiana both snap out of their trance back to reality as they stare at Dustin at the front door, stepping deeper inside the house.

Dustin. Juicy said as her lips tremble.

Good you remember me my sweet Juicy. You've always been my favorite. Dustin said.

When he spoke it freaked Tatiana and Juicy out. He had no lips and it made it seem as if he was smiling at them when he wasn't. His teeth were stained dark yellow. His eyes were blood shot red and watery because he had no eye lids and could not blink. His nose had been burnt completely off.

I miss the both of you so much. They let me out of jail early. I got paroled early for good behavior. He said then laughs. Hahaha! Eleven years is a long time to be apart from my girls. Dustin said as he steps deeper into the house looking at Juicy to Tatiana.

Noooo! I'll never let you touch me or my sister again! Tatiana shouted as she aims the shotgun and fought back her tears as thoughts about all the times he came into her room and raped them both play in her mind.

Her arms tremble as she held the shotgun. Her facial expression was balled up in in rage mixed with pain as she pulls the trigger.

'Boom!' The Shotgun roars but not before the Stalker aim and throw the black paddle covered in little metal spikes.

It hits the shotgun to the side, causing her to miss her shot. The Stalker charges at her and grabs the shotgun and tries to pull it out of her hand. Tatiana refuses to let the shotgun go as she grips it with both hands. She swung her feet upwards kicking him in the balls.

Ughhhh! He groaned in pain as he bends over but didn't release the shotgun.

He digs in his pocket with his left hand and pulls out the electric Taser as Tatiana sent her right knee crashing into his chin.

Ughhhh! He groaned in pain.

Juicy help me! She shouted as the Stalker places the electric Taser onto her stomach and presses the button sending four hundred volts of electricity through her body.

Ahhhh! Ahhhh! She hollered in excruciating pain as her body shook uncontrollably and white foam comes out the corners of her mouth and she falls backwards onto the floor.

"I owe you a lot worst for the beautiful makeover you gave me eleven years ago. You made me look like a monster!" The Stalker shouted as he stood over her body watching her go in to convulsions, shaking and twitching.

"I made you look like the monster you are inside." Tatiana managed to say while foam and spit flew out her mouth that she was choking on.

The Stalker stares at her. He looks like a demon as he bends down and pressed the electric Taser against her forehead, shocking her once more. He watches her body twitch then removes the Taser as her world went black and she was unconscious.

"I got plans for you Tatiana, it will be just like old times, I waited too long to just kill you fast. No I won't rush this at all." He said as he kicks her in the ribcage then kicks the shotgun and it slides across the floor into the kitchen and he bends down and picks up the paddle. Juicy stood frozen in a daze watching everything.

Pain ran down her right thigh as she lost control of her bowels out of fear. She felt as if she was eight years old all over again and Dustin controlled her life and body and she was helpless to do anything about it. The Stalker walks over to Shanelle's body that looked broken and twisted up. He raises the paddle high.

"You I don't need." He said.

"Noooo!" Juicy screams as loud as she could.

Startling the Stalker, he turns his head and stares in her direction with the paddle still raised high.

"Don't hurt my friend or sister. It's me you really want!" She yelled.

The Stalker twisted his head in a weird angle. Juicy couldn't stand to look at his horrifying face. His blood shot red eyes, his mouth with no lips, his raw flesh.

"You're right! I want Tatiana, but it's you who I despise. Come give daddy a kiss." The stalker said in a voice that sent chills down her spine.

"If you want it" "Juicy said as she back pedals. "Then come and get it!"She screamed and took off for the front door and runs outside in hopes of leading him away from her sister and Tatiana.

"Noooo!" The stalker yelled. "I waited too long to get my hands on you, just for you to think you can escape me, you're mines!" He shouted as he snatches the leather sex mask out of Shanelle's hand and puts it on while he takes off running.

"Help me! Help me!" Juicy screams repeatedly as she runs down the block.

It was 3:00 a.m. in the morning. The streets were dark and quite for a New York night. The long street lights shine on each block. Juicy's heart races as she looks back and could see the Stalker chasing her at full speed with the paddle in his hand and the creepy sex mask on his face.

"Help! Somebody help me please!"She screams until her voice was sore and hoarse.

She ran two blocks barefooted and turns the corner then sees the Beach 60th Street train station and a glances of hope raise deep inside her soul.

'*Maybe somebody will be there to help me or the guy in the toll both.*' She thought to herself as she continues to run and was out of breath.

She could hear the Stalker's footsteps quickly closing in on her. She ran up the long flight of stairs then stops and bends over to catch her breath. She looks at the toll booth and panic consumes her body when she sees that the toll both was empty.

'*Oh yea ever since the damn M.T.A. came out with that metro card machine, there's only a few train stations that actually have people working in them.*' She said out loud to herself.

She looks behind herself to see the Stalker running up the flight of stairs.

Juicy you belong to me! I miss my sweet Juicy box. It will be just like old times. Come to daddy! He shouted.

Noooo! Juicy screamed in horror and started crying all over again.

'*God help me! Please save me!*' She said with tears running down her cheeks and her facial expression twists up in despair mixed with sadness.

'No Juicy, don't you give up yet.' She told herself then took off running once again.

She ducks up under the turnstile and ran up another flight of stairs to the train platform. She looks around praying that somebody, anybody was around to help her, but it was completely deserted.

⬜I got you now!⬜She heard the Stalker⬜s voice boom.

She jumps out of fear and turns around to see him smiling a twisted grin through the sex mask as he stood on the platform. She back pedals and starts crying hysterically with just the thoughts of him forcing himself inside her, like he used to do. Juicy lowers her and knew it was over. She had nowhere to run. They were twenty feet high up in the air on a train platform. She lifts up her head and her eyes open up wide and a slight smile spread across her face as she sees a train pulling into the station, she took off running again as the train came to a full stop and the doors open. She ran onto the train.

⌐You will not escape me Juicy, eleven years is a long wait to taste what⌐s mine!⌐The Stalker shouted as he enters the train just as the doors were closing and it pulls off.

⌐Help me! Please help me! A man is chasing me and he⌐s trying to rape and kill me!⌐ Juicy screamed as she sees two men, one Afro-American and the other Caucasian sitting on the train looking as if they were heading to work at a construction site, and a Chinese couple holding and kissing each other.

The Afro-American construction worker stood up out his seat. Juicy ran to him.

⌐Help me please!⌐She cried.

The construction worker looks down at her bare feet that once were brown but now a dirty charcoal color then he looks at the tears streaming down her face.

⌐Miss calm down, who⌐s after you?⌐He asked.

⌐I am!⌐The Stalker said as he enters the cart.

The two construction workers look down at the end of the cart to see a tall slim built of a man dressed in all black with a black leather sex mask on and a paddle in his hand. Both of the construction workers laugh.

⬜I know Halloween is in a few days, but this must be some kind of joke. You⬜re a fucking freak. Leave this young lady alone asshole!⬜ The Caucasian one yelled as he became more confident by his size and seeing how skinny framed the body of the Stalker was.

Halloween is every day for me.⬜ The Stalker said then removes the leather sex mask off his face and stuffs it in to his back pocket.

⬜Holy shit! Ahhhh! Ahhhh!⬜Both of the construction workers scream, so did the Chinese couple that was sitting down, as they all look at what should be a man⬜s face but wasn⬜t.

It⬜s like a demon or something straight out of hell. His yellow stained teeth made it seem as if he was smiling at them because he had no lips, he had no eye lids, no ears or hair on his head. His face looked like raw meat.

⬜Chill man, I don⬜t want any problems with you.⬜ One of the construction workers said.

"It's too late for that Mr. Hero." The Stalker replied and pulls out the .22-Caliber handgun from his pocket that he took from Tatiana earlier that night.

He aims and squeezes the trigger twice sending two bullets dead center into one of the construction worker's head, killing him instantly. His body drops like a ton of bricks onto the dirty train floor. Then he sent two bullets into the chest of the next construction worker.

"Ugghhaaa!" He groaned in pain while holding his chest and coughing up blood as he fell sideways onto the trains hard plastic seats.

The Stalker puts back on his leather sex mask.

"Ahhhh! Ahhhh!" The Chinese couple screams and stood frozen in their seat holding each other praying he would go away.

Juicy had seen more than enough and did what she did best, run. She ran to the next end of the train car and opens the door that lead to another car. She walks through it and looks back through the glass door windows on the train door and cried. The Stalker walks up to the Chinese couple and swung the paddle.

FETISH

"Ahhhh! Ugghhaa! Ahhhh!"The Chinese couple hollered and screams in excruciating pain as the paddle cracks the man's head and crushes the woman's cheek bones.

The spikes got stuck inside the woman's face. The stalker yanks it away, ripping the skin off the woman's cheek and neck, sending pieces of her face along with blood flying onto the trains side windows and walls. The Stalker swung again and the bones in the man's arm could be heard breaking in half.

"Ahhhhhh!"The Chinese couple scream until they were too weak and in pain.

They couldn't scream anymore. The Stalker continues to swing and beat them until they stop moving and every bone in their bodies were crushed, then he beats them some more until there was nothing more than a pile of flesh and meat mixed with pieces of clothes. Blood and guts ooze onto the trains floor.

Juicy's body shook in horror. She back pedals and realizes she was in the first car of the train with nowhere to run. She could see the Stalker clearly covered in blood and whipping it off his sex mask and shirt. He looks up and grins when he stared into Juicy's eyes.

FETISH

I'm coming for you. He said in a creepy voice as he walks through the doors into the next train car.

Help me somebody, please help! She cried out.

There's no one to help you Juicy. You're mines, you always been my little fetish. The Stalker said as he walks toward her.

The train came to a full stop making him lose his balance for a second. The train doors open and Juicy realize they had reached the next stop, Beach 90th Street. She ran off the train, but the Stalker got off the train at the same time as her, blocking her way down the platform to the stairs, the only exist.

I am tired of playing this cat and mouse game with you. You're making me very upset, to the point I'm thinking about killing you just to make me smile then fuck your dead corpse. The Stalker said as he steps closer.

Juicy cried as she continues to walk backwards and looks around for a way to get away, but there was none. She was twenty feet high on a train platform. She stumbles when she bumps into a black melt trash can.

⬛I⬛l kill myself and jump over this rail and fall twenty feet to my death before I let you touch me!⬛ Juicy screamed with tears in her eyes.

⬛Go ahead, I⬛l just scoop what⬛s left of you off the street and still fuck you!⬛ The Stalker said as he looks and charges at her with the wooden paddle raised high as if he was playing baseball and about to hit a homerun.

Juicy turns around and grabs the heavy melt trash can and swung it, just as he was arm reach of her unexpectedly hitting him in the side.

⬛Ugghhaa!⬛ The Stalker groans in pain as he lost his balance and stumbles sideways.

⬛You will never touch my fucking body again!⬛ Juicy shouted and swung the heavy metal trash can over and over hitting him in the head and ribs.

He tries to put up his hands up to block her blows, but it did little to nothing to protect him.

⬛Ugghhaa! Ugghhh!⬛He screams in pain and got a glance of Juicy⬛s eyes when his head wasn⬚ spinning and sees pure rage he had never seen before.

⬚You raped me throughout my childhood, took away my innocence, now you want to do the same to me as an adult!⬚Juicy screamed as tears stream down her cheek.

Her facial expression was twisted up in heartache mixed with anger as flashbacks of Dustin beating her when she said no and taking her goods anyway, and her mother not caring or believing, and let it go on for years.

⬚You damn child molester! You fucking monster!⬚The louder she screamed the harder she swung the metal trash can.

The Stalker was leaning on the rail of the platform hollering in pain.

⬚Ugghhh! Ahhhh! Ahhhh!⬚

⬚You dirty piece of shit!⬚Juicy screams and swung with all her might, knocking him in the face.

He flips over the rail. Juicy stops her attack and looks over the rail to see him hanging on the rail with one hand. It was the only thing keeping him from a twenty foot fall to the concrete street below.

FETISH

"Juicy help me! Help me! Help your father don't let me fall." The Stalker said as he felt his hand slipping.

"You're not my father! I'll help you alright!" Juicy said while wiping her tears and bends over and sunk her teeth into his fingers.

"Ahhhhhh! Ahhhhhh!" He hollered in pain and lost his grip and falls.

"Ahhhhhh! Juicyyyyyy!" He screams as he continues to fall twenty feet and hits the hard concrete.

Juicy looks over the rail to see his body stretched out in a twisted broken position and blood was everywhere.

'Thank you God.' Juicy said as she walks down the stairs to the main train station and went to a pay phone and called the police.

Tatiana's head was spinning and she tries and to say as less as possible to the police officers as possible. She refuses to go the hospital and receive any medical treatment and was becoming more and more frustrated with the police officer interrogating them, as if they were the suspects.

Juicy sat next to her sister on the couch in their living room with two detectives standing over them.

We have both of your statements, along with the other woman Shanelle who went to the hospital, but your stories aren't adding up. For one, there was no body at Beach 90th Street. If someone fell over the rail off the platform twenty feet, they're not going to be able to get up and leave and I seriously doubt someone will come along and move the body. There wasn't even a blood stain, are you sure you seen the man fall? An overweight Caucasian detective asked with a receding hairline.

Yes, why would I lie? Juicy said while fighting back her tears and couldn't understand why the detectives didn't believe her.

Ummm, sure okay, this is kind of a weird case. They have a unit with two detectives running it, Alexis Lovett and Lauren Pitman. Maybe they will take this unbelievable case, who knows. The Detective said sarcastically while writing down notes in a small black pad in his hand.

Why in the fuck won't you believe my sister? She said he fell over the fucking platform, so it's fucking true. She never lies even when she should!" Tatiana shouted as she stood up.

"Watch your damn tone. First off you have a record for assault charges and prostitution and all your tricks end up murdered. We have bodies in a hotel that you, your sister and Shanelle are the only eyewitnesses to is what lead me to the conclusion that this is a whore house and y'all could have easily set all your dates up to get robbed, but took it too far!" The detective shouted back.

Tatiana's facial expression balls up with anger as she did her best to hold her tongue. It took everything in her power to not curse the Detective out.

"Why won't you believe us? It was Dustin Favor, my mother's old boyfriend who murdered all those people." Juicy said while crying.

"Juicy don't explain anything more to them, they already judged us without knowing who we really are and don't care. Get the fuck out of my house!" Tatiana shouted.

˹That˼s fine with me.˼The detective said as he and his partner made their way to the front door then he stops and turns around.

˹There˼s only one problem with your story ladies.˼The overweight detective said as he turns back around and walks out the front door.

˹Yea and what is that?˼ Tatiana said with an attitude.

The Detective turns back around and stares at them both.

˹You both said it was Dustin Favor who did the murders.˼The Detective replied.

˹Yes we know how Dustin looks and sound we can pick his ugly ass face out in a crowd of people in the street.˼Tatiana replied while grilling the detective.

˹That˼s nice and all, but Dustin Favor was killed three years ago during a gang rape in prison.˼The detective said then walks to his car leaving Juicy and Tatiana standing in there house doorway trembling in fear with their mouths wide open.

Fetish II

Juicy had spent the whole day in the hospital visiting Kandy-Cola who was fighting for her life. One of the bullets had pierced her lung, but the doctors were able to get her in a stable condition, the rest was up to her body to heal. Juicy steps out the hospital, the night air sent a slight breeze down her back making a sweet chill travel down her spine. She smiled when she seen her best friend Marvin's grey Nissan Maxima in the hospital parking lot. She walks over and hops in the passenger seat shutting the door behind her.

Hey Juicy booty. Marvin said as he starts up the car and pulls off.

Hey Marvin, thanks for coming to pick me up. Tatiana's head still hurts too bad to be driving so I took the train. The ride to the city from Far Rockaway is like an hour. She said while staring at him.

Marvin was a slim handsome man in his early twenties and what most women would call a square or nerd. He wore big glasses that look like bifocals. Most women would pay him no mind or give him the time of day because he was the type of man you could walk all over.

⬚You should have seen this coming Juicy. I have been telling you to leave your sister and friends alone.⬚ Marvin said while driving.

⬚Schmmp!⬚Juicy sucks her teeth.

⬚You really want to start this now. There⬚s so much you don⬚t know and I have to tell you. Tatiana saved my life as a child from my mother⬚s boyfriend. This would have happened even if I wasn⬚t running the streets with her, because he⬚s free out there somewhere.⬚Juicy replied.

But you told me the detectives said he was killed in jail. So how could it be him?⬚ Marvin responded.

⬚I don⬚t know, but I do know what I seen with my own eyes and my sister seen him too. I over think the situation sometimes as it keeps playing in my mind and I wonder how he kept finding us at all the addresses to the dates we went on. New York City is very big, but it was as if he knew.⬚As the words left Juicy⬚s mouth she turns her head slightly and looks in the back seat of the car and sees a Mac Laptop the same color as the one that was in the house with the guys that ran a train on her and Tatiana.

She stretched her neck to get a better look and what she sees behind the driver seat made her eyes open up wide as her mind puts together some of the pieces to the missing puzzle and it all became clear as she stares at the leather sex mask and paddle.

It was you! You told him all the addresses we were at? You were the only person I told, but why? Juicy asks with a confuse look on her face and she starts to cry.

Marvin stops at a red light and turns and faces her with a devilish smile on his face. A smile she had never seen him use before.

Ugghhaa! Ahhhh! Juicy groaned in pain as she foams at the mouth as Marvin presses the electric Taser against her neck sending four hundred volts of electricity through her body.

Why? Was the only word she was able to mumble as her body went into convulsions and her world goes dark then she went unconscious.

FETISH

"Mmmm!" Juicy moans and felt weak.

She rubs her neck and swears she could hear her mother's voice. Even though she hadn't spoken to her mother in years she could never forget her voice. She tried to stand up and bumps her head on a metal bar and realizes she was in an oversized dog cage. She grabs the front cage bars as she panics. The room she was in was pitched black, but she could make shapes of some of the things as she tries to figure out where she was at. She turns her head and could see another cage.

"Marvin!" She shouted, but he didn't respond as he lay twisted up in the cage next to her unconscious.

"You will take him from me again! Not this time you little bitch!" Juicy heard a voice shout.

"Mom is that you!" Juicy replied as a door a few feet from her opens up shinning a white bright light into the room.

Juicy's facial expression balls up as she quickly puts up her forearms to block the bright light. She could see a silhouette of a shape of an overweight woman in the door way.

FETISH

"You will never take him from me this time I'll make sure of it! Do you hear me?" The woman screamed.

"That is you, Mom?" Juicy replied and then her heart race as another figure steps into the doorway.

Tears stream down her face as her body trembles as the Stalker stood next to her mother and removes the leather sex mask off his face showing his hideous of a monster face.

"I told you that you would be mines, my sweet Juicy." He said in a creepy voice that made Juicy lose control of her bladder and pee on herself.

He then turns to Juicy's mother Heather and held her by the waist and kisses her.

"You won't take him again from me." Heather said as her and the Stalker stop kissing.

"Noooo! Noooo! Tatiana! Tatiana, help me! Help me! Noooo!" Juicy screamed while crying as the Stalker and Heather shut the door making it completely pitched black, as they walk towards her"

FETISH

Other Novels by Shameek A. Speight:

Novels Coming In 2013:

A Child of a CrackHead IV
The Pleasure of Pain III
The S.N. Killer II
BornBangers II
For The Love of My Sister

Made in the USA
Columbia, SC
10 August 2021